CW01521487

Mary Grayer Clarke has been reading since the age of three. Her first publication was in the *Newfoundland Magazine* in 1984. She was also involved with the publication of her husband's technical books in the late 1990s. Mary started writing seriously when she joined a Creative Writing course, but it was not until moving to Cornwall in 2020, prior to the first Covid-19 lockdown, that she completed a novel started in 2004. *Dark Regressions* was published in 2023, the sequel *Dark Revenge* in 2024 and *Dark Resurgence* in August 2024. So a *Dark Trilogy* was accomplished. Mary firmly believes that every cloud has a silver lining and age is just numbers.

I dedicate this book to the memory of my father, Thomas Vizard.

Mary Grayer Clarke

A Miscellany of Odds & Ends

AUSTIN MACAULEY PUBLISHERS®

LONDON * CAMBRIDGE * NEW YORK * SHARJAH

A CIP catalogue record for this title is available from the British Library.

ISBN 9781037108730 (Paperback)
ISBN 9781037108747 (ePub e-book)

www.austinmacauley.com

First Published 2025
Austin Macauley Publishers Ltd®
1 Canada Square
Canary Wharf
London
E14 5AA

Acknowledgements

It is with enormous gratitude that I thank Austin Macauley Publishers for their consistent support with the four novels they have accepted from me. The final published book far exceeds my expectations and I have only praise for every department. The fact that I no longer consider myself 'a rookie' is because of the members of various teams, who show consideration and patience. Thank you one and all.

To my son and his wonderful wife, Toby and Kay, my love and thanks are with you forever. Without them to encourage and help me, whenever I need help sending information, I would never have had the courage to try to get my writings published.

Thank you, my friends at Marchwood Writers Circle. The group meetings and reading my work to the others helped to give confidence.

Of course my thanks and memories are always with my parents, Gladys and Thomas Vizard. I was born two years before WW2, but at that time and throughout my childhood, they were there for me. My mother's maiden name was Grayer, which is why I use it in the author's name. I have dedicated this book to my dad as the one in our family to act and write, but my mum was the one who read to me from a very early age whilst I looked at the page and got to understand printed words.

Finally, thank you to everyone who has chosen to read these stories.

Table of Contents

An Introduction from the Author

Short Stories – I never could manage to write in a compact enough manner to be able to consider my stories short. This was probably due to the fact that I always prefer to read a novel with depth and characters. I positively cannot read romance or bland family sagas either. Thus, the type of stories I wished to tell were undoubtedly guided by what I personally liked to read.

Then I joined a creative writing course.

Certainly, the best thing I could have done, for apart from anything else, I had to produce an assignment at the end of each term, to obtain a percentage mark, detailed comments from the tutor and ten credits towards the 365 required to gain the MA qualification.

This assignment had to be a piece of no more than 2000 words, together with a Statement of Aims (500 words maximum) which was, in fact, a self-critique and description of the work handed in for marking. If you are interested in writing, try to produce a critique in less than 500 words, believe me, it is harder than you can imagine. For starters, you must state where the idea for your assignment was conceived. Then the sources of support (i.e. things learnt in class, lectures given by the tutor, or perhaps, the influence of work of other authors). Areas of intention follow this, which effectively is a breakdown of your piece. I learnt that the more quotes I could fit into this section, the higher the mark I was likely to achieve.

Later, I was encouraged to try poetry. For this assignment, three poems needed to be produced, each with a critique of no more than 250 words. Now, I am not much of a poetry reader and must confess my preference is that it should first rhyme, then scan and preferably be humorous (Pam Ayres variety). Wordsworth always did have the same effect on me as Shakespeare. Now, don't get me wrong, the stories of the great William Shakespeare are superb tales of darkness, even the funny ones, but I always preferred *'Lamb's Tales'* of Shakespeare to the poetic writing of *'The Bard'*. That's fine, just a personal opinion, to each his own, but nevertheless, those opinions definitely dictate what is produced by any individual. But that is enough of my experiences, so on to the first story in this book.

The First Letter

To: Ma, Pa and my six siblings, June 1983

It's just not fair!

She talks on the thing for hours. It goes peep-peep and there she is, sitting on the stairs and yacking away. Usually, she rubs my tummy or scratches my ears at the same time, so I don't mind. But why should she mind if I try to talk to somebody too?

I will admit I was a little bit clumsy and pulled the darned thing onto the floor, and of course, I can't make *brrrs* with the roundy-roundy thing like she does. Well, Newfies have got rather large paws, haven't they? I just thought that if I tried chewing the bit she talks into, I might get her to hear me and talk to me from work.

Gosh, you should have heard her go on and on about damaging her precious telephone handset. You would have thought it was more important than *me*.

Doesn't she realise how bored I get on my own while she is having fun at work? I am here for four whole hours and although I do have plenty of toys and things like bones, a Newfie gets fed up with the same old things day after flipping day!

To make it worse, she went away two weeks ago and left me with her ex and O'Henry his St Bernard. I hope she doesn't go away often. I don't like going there.

St Bernards are bigger than Newfoundlands and rougher. I was completely exhausted by the end of the week, my dear. However, she did stay at home with me for a whole week after that and I sort of missed her today and wanted to tell her on the phone to come home to me *now*.

Oh well! You can't win 'em all and humans are such unpredictable creatures.

Love and licks from PG Wodehouse (Portadurn Sea King)

A Ghost's Story

"God, I'm bored!"

What's the matter with them, anyway? They can't all be blind, surely.

I've been walled up in this bloody cupboard for the last two hundred years.

I've knocked and tapped. I even trained myself to indulge in a little telekinesis but they just don't seem to notice. Not even the old woman. Mind you, I think she did see me just before that heart attack.

There's only been old Joe the caretaker since she died.

I am so bored!

Could do with some young life here, a boy preferably. I like little boys, always did. That's how I came to be walled up.

But…that's another story.

Well, how would you like to be walled up with no one to speak to and no one to haunt?

Old Joe doesn't count, he's always drunk anyway, wish I was too.

They put a heavy dresser in front of the cupboard when they walled me in. That's no problem to me, of course, I just glide through it. That's one of the things I *can* do.

I just float around, stuck, not able to move on.

Did you know ghosts can't sleep? Not like live bodies do. I have to get back in my corpse to relax.

But there's only a certain amount of time I want to spend in the cupboard behind that bloody dresser.

My corpse is now a decomposed heap of bones and space is small.

I could only sit with my knees up. Talk about cramped! Bastards!

I could stand up though, and that's how I finally died, trying desperately to free myself. But the doors on that cupboard were at least an inch thick.

It must have been the smell of my bleeding fingers that first attracted the rats.

They ate me alive. Ugh! I can still feel them nibbling my toes now.

14

Sometimes, I reach down to knock the filthy beasts away but, of course, I just go through.

Two hundred bloody years!

Nobody's ever even tried to move the dresser, wouldn't believe it, would you?

Hang on, was that the door? Listen!

"Are you the caretaker, sir?"

"Yeah."

"Police, can we come in, please?"

"Wa'for?"

"We have reason to believe that a murder's been committed and the body is concealed on these premises. Here's our warrant for the search. We'll start by moving that friggin' great dresser."

Nightmare Remembered

She was beautiful, her long legs stretched towards the retreating tide line. A deep natural tan that could only have been achieved by a mixture of salt water and sunshine. I thought she probably spent a great deal of time sailing, which would account for the taut, immaculately shaped body.

She was wearing what appeared to be a white bikini with a sleeveless tee shirt over it, covering her superb breasts, which although she was lying on her back, were still large and firm. They didn't appear to spread like breasts of this size usually do and as I stared down at her, the left one appeared to undulate independently and without any other movement on the part of the woman.

I gazed at her from the top of the sand dune without moving for about twenty minutes, testosterone pulsing through my system like a tsunami. I desperately wanted to be down there with her. I would only talk with her and find out her name. Perhaps I would arrange to take her to dinner one night.

But she is so beautiful, way out of my sphere. I was always rather shy around girls and my previous contact with them occurred in the local dance hall and an occasional trip to Hammersmith Palais. Even then, I quite often ended up with the less proficient dancers, feeling sorry for them. And in any case, I invariably delayed so long before asking someone to dance that the best ones were already on the floor. It was a stupid state of affairs, as at the time, I was receiving lessons from an excellent teacher and, in all honesty, should have been on the floor with the best of them.

So, you can see how difficult it was for me to approach this beautiful woman on the beach. Eventually, gathering my scattered thoughts and getting my body under control, plus some degree of courage, I went down the side of the dune towards this magnificent specimen of womanhood.

Apparently, she had not heard my approach, perhaps she was sound asleep, so I lowered myself quietly onto the soft sand next to her and, propping myself on one elbow, gazed at her, close up now.

The left breast appeared to move of its own accord again, just a gentle ripple.

Then, she opened her eyes and gasped as she saw me, at once rolling away and drawing her body into a sitting foetal position.

"What the hell do you think you are doing?" she said in a whispery voice that made me more apprehensive than I would have felt had she shouted.

I apologised for startling her, introduced myself and assured her it was not my habit to approach a woman on her own. I went on to explain how I had seen her and how I felt compelled to speak.

"Will you please have dinner with me tonight?" I asked.

Much to my surprise, she agreed. She told me her name was Angelica but that her friends called her Angel and as she was having dinner with me that night, I had better consider myself a friend, for the time being at least.

We met that night at the Country Club, where I knew the cuisine to be superb. We ate our food with which we drank two bottles of wine, but to this day, I cannot remember *what* we ate. We looked into each other's eyes and touched fingertips across the table. It was electric.

"Why did you agree to join me here?" I asked.

She gave a secretive smile and sparks seemed to fly between two pairs of deep brown eyes as we gazed at each other. "I am very choosy about the men with whom I keep company. They need to have that extra 'something' which automatically attracts me. Only I know what that is and I don't intend to tell you my secret. You are special, you not only saw and wanted me but also came down to me. And that's enough of that subject for now."

We finished our meal with coffee and liqueurs, rising from time to time to dance on the small square provided for diners. The band could hardly have compared with Joe Loss or Victor Sylvester, their timing being somewhat haywire, but the slow music provided an excuse to hold each other close.

Angel said she lived quite close by and, of course, I walked her home. She stopped before a large Victorian house. I kissed her hand, then lightly on the lips. Her arms encircled my neck and we kissed, passionately now. Then, arms around each other, we entered the house together where she had the attic flat. The stairs were wide, and we ascended side by side to the third floor. However, when we reached the steps leading to the attic, I realised they were much narrower, the door to her flat opening almost directly off the top step. Angel preceded me and opened the door that she had apparently not bothered to lock.

We were in a small hallway tiled in grey and black squares of about 30 centimetres from which led four doors, each of which was painted black as were the surrounding frames. One door was on the left-hand wall with another opposite it and two were set about two metres apart on the wall facing the entrance. The walls were plain white and held no adornment of any description. It was cold and I remember shivering, but it was not just my body that felt the chill.

I hesitated, wanting to withdraw and retreat to the street again but Angel placed her hand on my arm, leading me through the second door from the left and I found myself in her bedroom. I assumed the others led to a bathroom, a living room and a kitchen but was never given the opportunity to discover if I was correct.

I gasped. This was a large room of roughly five metres square. It was carpeted in thick pure white carpet and between the two large windows was a bed. It was not just any bed, but a four-poster made of what looked like ebony, the posts carved with both cherubs and gargoyles. It was two metres wide and draped in white silk. The pillows were covered in black satin, and the sheets proved to be of the same material, but the heavy linen bedspread was incredible. Centred was a large pentagon and around it were all the signs of the zodiac, thickly embroidered in black silk. Like the hallway, the walls were painted pure white and etched in black, upon each of the other three walls were figures depicting occult orgies, of humans and animals.

When I turned to look at the woman who lived in this amazing place, for a moment I could not see her, then I realised she was on the bed. The spread was folded neatly to the end of the bed, and she was covered by a black satin sheet, which clung to her perfect body leaving little to the imagination. Without more ado, I discarded my clothes, leaving them in a heap on the floor and joined her on the bed.

I wanted to put my hand under the sheet to caress her body, but she would not allow it, so I stroked her long black hair and continued over her body with the sheet between us. Her right breast felt softly firm beneath my hand, and I ran my hand over her nipple to arouse it more. Again, I tried to slip my hand under the sheet and again she stopped me.

I continued running my hand over her hair, body, and legs, down the right side and up the left. I glanced down and the left breast seemed momentarily to have a life of its own. I reached for it, held it gently and squeezed softly, then I felt for the nipple and pressed it between my finger and thumb. It felt slightly strange. I repeated the action on her other breast…perfectly normal, it must be me. Again, I returned to the left breast, squeezed and the nipple seemed to leap in my hand. The whole breast seemed to move beneath the pressure of my hand and swiftly gripping the sheet, I flung it back. Her perfect body lay before me, Angel moaned and taking my right hand, placed it again on her breasts. Nervously, I favoured the right one for some time before I plucked up the courage to pleasure the left one similarly. I ran the palm of my hand over the smooth surface, closed my fingers, squeezed the plump hillock, and screamed as a hundred needles seemed to pierce the skin. It felt as though I had picked up a handful of wasps.

My hand was a sore and bloody mess, looking more as though I had crushed fine glass in my hand, it was also beginning to swell.

The breast I had clasped was a seething mass of wriggling wormlike creatures at each end of which, was a mouth filled with tiny sharp teeth. It appeared that they had dwelt within the left breast of this beautiful woman and had eaten their way through to bite the hand that dared to caress.

I screamed. "What are you, for God's sake?"

"That is an expression I do not allow to be used in this establishment." Angel still lay on her back and appeared to be perfectly normal. There was no sign of the worm things that had bitten my hand a few seconds ago. She was still that beautiful and perfect woman.

"Please, Angel, tell me why I am here, how I am special to you? Please! What can I do about my hand, it hurts?"

She swung her legs over the side of the bed and held her hand out towards me. "Come here to me, my special man."

I wasn't too happy about it but her hypnotic eyes drew me towards her. She gently took my injured right hand and laid it on her right breast, then pulling me to her, kissed my forehead. I was unable to escape her powers now and allowed my hand to roam her breast. The one which only seconds ago was a writhing mass was now quite normal. I stared at the appendage, realising it was in the same condition as when I had walked into this amazing residence.

Realising my surprise, Angel said, "I said you were special. Not every man can cause my worm-bug's teeth to retreat. I shall keep you, my special man."

I am not quite clear as to what happened next, I think we made love.

~~

19

When later, I awoke in that magic bed and looked towards where the door had previously stood, it was no longer there. I surveyed each wall in turn, no doors. *"Angel,"* I called and looked down at the bed, to my horror, she was no longer there, but where she had lain was a squirming mass of vicious little worms.

I rolled away, falling heavily onto the floor, waking both my wife and myself.

The hand on which I had been laying for some time began to release its pins and needles.

Putting on the light, my beloved wife peered down at me from the bed, her right breast there as it had always been. The other side was scarred from where that dreadful thing – whose name I still cannot bring myself to say aloud – had been removed, together with her left breast, in an attempt to prevent them from eating into other parts of her dear body.

~~~

Isn't it strange how some dreams stay with you whilst others disappear into an impenetrable fog never to be recalled?

Help Me!

George looked up at the shopping centre clock. *Gone half past four, cripes!* he thought, *Mum'll scalp me.*

The ten-year-old attended an after-school computer course that should have finished in time for him to be home by 4.30. Today, they had joined a chat line with some kids in the USA and the teacher had practically had to lever the class from their seats a full twenty minutes later than usual. By the time George and the other children had collected their coats, it was already near the time he usually arrived home.

It would take George a good twelve minutes to get home if he hurried, but he wasn't hurrying. He dawdled along, engrossed in an old computer magazine brought in by the teacher. *I'll have a laptop, so I can carry it around. I'll even take it to class with me and everyone will be jealous,* he thought. The daydream continued with, *George.com, the amazing internet company of the decade, started up by the schoolboy who became a millionaire.*

He realised the park gates were before him, which was when he looked at the clock tower. If he went past the park and crossed over at the other end, he would reach his road on the other side of the shopping centre. On the other hand, if he crossed the road here, he could save five minutes by cutting through the council estate.

Mum'd be mad at me if she knew I cut through the estate, George thought, *but I needn't tell her and I won't be so late.* He was not supposed to take that route on his own, but he'd been that way with his big brother, so it wasn't as though he'd get lost, and he'd save time.

Mind made up, George pressed the wait button on the traffic lights and waited impatiently for the green man to replace the red one.

The streets were quiet. The older kids would be around soon though, wouldn't they? It was a bit strange not to see anyone about on this estate. He shrugged and thought, *Never mind, nearly home.* George turned onto Niton

Road. Halfway down was a narrow cut that led directly into Ventnor Place, his road. When he had nearly reached it, a group of four boys squeezed through a dilapidated gate hanging by one hinge.

"Where d'you think you're goin'?" A boy of about fifteen placed himself in front of George.

"I…I'm on my way home," he stuttered, sounding as scared as he felt. *Oh shit! This is why I'm not supposed to come through here on my own,* he thought.

He stepped to the side, hoping to go around the group but they formed a circle around him.

"Wassat?" A boy of about his own age grabbed at the magazine, tearing it.

"Please! That's my computer magazine, don't tear it."

This was not a promising idea. The boy tore off the cover.

"Oops!" he said. "Looks like it's got ripped."

Another boy also clutched hold and between them, the two began to rip up the magazine.

George made a sudden grab, trying to recover his precious magazine, and the eldest boy cuffed him round the ear, making his head ring.

"Li'l jerks what reads abaht compu'ers needs to learn abaht real life. You don' live round 'ere, do yer? Live in Ventnor Place, do yer? You lot finks yer too good fer us. Le's teach 'im a lesson."

The speaker lunged at George again and he raised his fists, bravely trying to defend himself. His head flicked from side to side, desperately dodging the blows from the large hands of his attacker.

The next blow knocked him to the ground. He shouted for help but found it difficult to speak between the kicks to his body, which were knocking the breath out of him.

The boys stepped back whilst George, lying on his side in a foetal position, tried to get his breath back. It hurts so much.

I'll be really late now, he thought, *Mum'll be really worried. I wish I'd gone the long way like I'm supposed to.*

But it was too late for that now. George heard the sound of smashing glass and saw that the biggest boy now held a wine bottle from which, with some sign of expertise, he had smashed the base, leaving a jagged edge. Fear gripped George, fists and feet were bad enough, but this broken bottle would cut him, make him bleed. Blood scared him, made him feel sick. They still had him caught in the middle, with no room to run and no way to escape.

"Help me, please."

It was a quiet call for help, through bruised and swollen lips.

A woman with a pushchair passed by on the other side of the road.

George cried out again. Louder this time.

"Help me!"

Maybe she didn't hear me, he thought.

She had heard him but thought better of interfering with the activities of those particular troublemakers. She prayed she would be able to move away from the estate before her baby grew to school age.

A man tidying his garden swiftly packed up and retreated indoors, where he peeped between curtains. Then he let them drop and went into the kitchen to make a cup of tea.

Fred Wilkins, walking Spot his Jack Russell, thought, *If I was ten years younger, I'd sort the little bastards out. Trouble is, if I laid a finger on 'em they'd probably have me in court for abuse, never mind what they're doing to the little lad.*

"I don't know what the country's coming to, Spot," he spoke aloud to his dog. "The bloody gov'ment ought to send 'em to a boot camp, they need someone to put a boot up 'em." Fred made a croaking noise that could have been a laugh or a cough. If he saw a policeman, he would get them to look into the fracas, but unfortunately, policemen on the beat were like hen's teeth around here.

In the block of flats at the corner, there were watchers. An elderly couple sat on the tiny balcony drinking tea and enjoying the sun.

"Bloody kids," said the husband.

The wife responded. "They're just children, dear, boys will be boys," as she continued to knit yet another sweater for her ten-year-old grandson. She had not yet realised that he would rather wear a designer sweatshirt than 'a nice hand-knitted garment' from his grandmother.

From behind entirely unnecessary net curtains on the fifth floor, Alice watched the proceedings through her father's binoculars. This was a bit of excitement. She fancied Gary like crazy. He was always the one in charge and one day, he was going to be like the Kray brothers. His two younger brothers, Jase and Tom, worshipped him and would follow like sheep. And she was going to be Gary's moll. She would wear designer clothes, all the latest styles, go to the biggest nightclubs and take expensive drugs. Gary would probably have his own club, perhaps she would be the lead singer there. Alice's dreams were like George's, just dreams, but unlike him, she was dreaming from the safety of home.

Old Flora peeped out at the scuffle from a first-floor window overlooking the cut and shivered. She kept to herself, going out only when she was sure the local children were at school. Her daughter visited every day. Carol was a good girl. Flora knew some of the occupants of these flats had windows broken and nasty things pushed through their letterboxes. That was why she kept to herself. If people didn't know her, they couldn't take exception to her…could they? She thought she ought to telephone the police but that was getting involved, then the media would be round and she would lose that precious privacy.

~~

Meanwhile, poor George was pretty much a bleeding mess. His attackers had dragged him into the cut.

"Right, yer've got till I count ter ten, then we're after yer."

"Yah could of 'ad up ter twen'y but 'e 'asn't got 'is Nikes on."

The others laughed but the speaker was silenced with a vicious punch in the solar plexus from their leader.

"Shurup or yer'll get done over too. Nah. Go fer it, nerd! One, two," the counting got faster, and George stumbled away.

As he tried to run, he was jabbed with the jagged glass bottle, wherever his attacker could jab.

I'm bleeding. George was holding his arm now, feeling the sticky blood warm on his fingers. He tried to run but he hurt so much from the kicks to his body. He didn't know it, but two ribs were broken and his right shoulder had been dislocated. He couldn't breathe very well. Every breath was like a knife being stuck in his chest and coming out through his back. His shoulder wouldn't seem to move properly, it hurt but not like his chest. It was more like being thumped with a big stick. A different hurt. Another hurt.

The irregular bleeping of a police car alerted the boys.

"Pigs comin'."

The leader gave a final vicious jab of the broken bottle into George's arm, where it cut into a main artery and the four boys made off in the opposite

24

direction. Then, with an air of innocence, they climbed over the fence into the park in search of more mischief.

Flora could see the young boy was bleeding profusely and picked up the telephone receiver, pressing the number nine three times. She spoke shakily, out of breath, "Police, quick. Four big boys are setting about a younger one and he's bleeding. Niton Road. In the cut. Tell them to hurry."

Before she could be drawn into giving her name, she replaced the receiver and sat down, shaking. She would telephone Carol later and tell her all about it. Carol would know if she'd done the right thing.

The two officers allocated the task of investigating the telephone call, put down the newspapers they were reading and turned the car out of the relative peace of a group of lock-up garages. The tyres squealed as they raced round the corner towards the estate.

"Turn the alarm on, Charlie," the driver instructed.

They reached Niton Road and peered down the cut, there was no sign of the boys.

"Another fuckin' hoax call," the driver sounded fed up.

"They said it was an old lady called," said his partner, "perhaps we'd better have a look around, Jim."

"Charlie, me old mate, if you want to go walkies around this estate, then bloody well do it. I'll let you out but sure as hell I'm not coming with you."

Jim slowed the car but when his partner shook his head accelerated again. They drove through the estate, returning to Niton Road, which now showed no sign of any boys, and sped away to more interesting pastimes.

~~

Holding the cut on his arm as tightly as possible, George struggled to his feet once again and slowly made his way towards home. He reached the door and rang the bell. *Where was everybody today?* No one answered. "Mum!" George cried feebly and collapsed in a heap in the corner of the porch.

His worried mother had set off in search of her son at quarter to five, following the route he was supposed to take home until she reached a now empty and locked school. She returned by the same route, nodding distractedly in response to the *good afternoon* from the man walking his Jack Russell to the park.

Her son was curled up in the corner of the porch when she got home again. His face, body and clothes were red. She screamed, "George! Georgie darling! Speak to me."

But George didn't speak then, or ever again.

The Chaperone

It was Lamas when first she heard his voice. The voice that stood out above all others on the 'airwaves' by virtue of its quality of tone and content. She spoke with him for only a short three minutes but in that space of time, I knew her destiny would be inexorably entwined with his, by hook or by crook.

He was known as 'King of Power', she as 'Lady Mystery'. These were their 'handles' on the illegal CB radio bands.

A month passed before she spoke to him again on the CB radio and this time they talked for much longer. During this communication, she claimed to be a witch with power over the minds of others.

His admirers left him an entire channel to himself whenever he desired this unusual privilege of the airwaves. It became known as 'The King of Power Hour'.

His enemies listened for interesting titbits and rudely interrupted him, according to the subject upon which he was expounding.

One evening that I recall clearly, there was a deep discussion between the two of them concerning Extra Sensory Perception. The atmosphere was charismatic but I felt an unpleasant sensation sweep through my body and shivered.

They spoke together most evenings after that, until eventually, a meeting was arranged. I was ordered to accompany him and dared to voice my inclinations about the visit and opinion of her – very unwise. It was to ensure my future as a 'chaperone'.

~~

We visited her home in Gosforth in September and it was only then that her real name was disclosed as Vera Dennis.

The house was in the midst of a terrace on an estate of exactly similar dwellings and she came out to greet us carrying her three-year-old daughter. After only ten minutes of this ill-behaved, spoiled brat who appeared to rule the household, I felt cheered. My husband had a low tolerance level and was no lover of children at the best of times. I felt that surely this would ensure it was the first and last visit to Gosforth but had, unfortunately, not taken the attraction and power of their personalities into account.

As we entered the house, a sixteen-year-old daughter was told to prepare lunch and make tea.

The three-year-old brat told another sister. "Get me a drink."

Receiving this, she then whinged, "I want my red jumper." When it was fetched she whined that she didn't want it. There was no argument, this brat got what she wanted.

They conversed avidly for several hours, his dark eyes under beetle brows gazing into green ones, like those of a cat. It was as though they were engulfed in a bubble containing only themselves.

She was certainly knowledgeable. She was prepared, only rarely slipping into her natural accent and speech patterns. She told how when expecting her last child, with five other daughters around her, she had studied and passed an examination in psychology. Her knowledge of drugs, was also extensive and she proudly declared that when she wanted to be rid of her husband for an evening, she gave him a *Brompton Cocktail* so that he would sleep. I took this for bravado at the time, but personal experience later proved it to be true.

By the time we left for the journey home, I realised without a doubt that the fight for my husband was on…one I really did not relish. This marriage for me had always been difficult but I'd believed in the sanctity thereof. He was a good provider and I had learnt to behave as was expected of me, to avoid being punished like a child and childlike, I was afraid of my 'Lord and Master'. I suppose, in retrospect, that no independence *could* be allowed me; control *had* to be tight for fear of losing it.

~~

By now, a year had passed and CB radios had become legal, thus decreasing the interest by leaps and bounds. This, however, did not mean contact between Benedict and Vera had ceased. We collected her and the brat regularly each

Saturday and took them wherever Benedict decreed. My job was to act as a chaperone and ultimately to prepare a meal for us all when we returned home. They talked and played chess while I did this and tried to amuse the obnoxious child. I think her husband, Bill, must have worked on Saturdays, for we rarely saw him.

~~

It was one Friday night when both of them were invited to dinner at our home, that first brought to mind how I might rid myself of her unwelcome presence. We had met Bill at their home but it was his first visit to ours.

At that time, we had a Pyrenean Mountain Dog. By no means are all Pyrenean dogs fierce and not easily controlled, but Satan lived up to her name, hating other animals and humans. However, *we* could mostly do as we pleased, which doesn't necessarily mean she always obeyed but at least she showed only pleasure in our company rather than her usual aggression. However, if visitors were expected, she had to be locked safely away. Benedict thought this was a wonderful trait. Satan's devotion to me lay in her doggy memory of my tender loving care when she was inflicted by Parvovirus and the hours I spent bathing her sores and soothing her. Satan always seemed to know instinctively what was in my mind and I often wished I could return the compliment.

But to return to that night. Dinner was finished and with the dishes stacked in the machine, we settled around the fire with coffee and liquors.

Later, Benedict took our visitors up to his Den, which contained his large model railroad. I, for some unaccountable reason, felt nervous. Then suddenly, thump! The door was flung back against the wall and in hurtled Satan. The dog went straight for Bill, her front paws on his shoulders knocking him backwards, where the edge of a desk brought him to a stop. Had she not been grabbed and pulled off by her master, Satan would have bitten straight into the jugular.

Pyrenean Mountain dogs are used to protect sheep, by fighting off bears and wolves. Consequently, they instinctively fight standing on their hind legs, attacking their adversaries with long sharp claws and biting for the throat.

Satan was speedily removed, and Benedict winked at me. Later, he boasted how he alone could have pulled the ferocious animal away from her conceived enemy. Laughing, he said, "Bill was so scared, did you see how white he went?

Stupid little man. How on earth did a clever woman like Vera come to marry a jerk like that?"

"She was probably pregnant," I responded derisively. Another mistake.

My teeth shook as Benedict's hand struck my face, palm one side, knuckles the other. Fool that I am, I should know by now to keep my thoughts to myself. Staggering to my feet, I wavered towards the door, wiping blood from my mouth.

"Where do you think you are going?"

He caught me by the shoulder and pushed me onto a chair.

"Your mouth will be the death of you," he said. "I'm sorry if I hurt you but I must say you asked for it. Vera is a brilliant person and I like having her around. She is capable of intelligent conversation and can play chess, neither of which you are capable of sustaining. It is a tragedy that she has to put up with that stupid creature and the poor woman has six daughters by him!"

Benedict sounded astounded by this fact. "That alone should tell you what an animal he must be. She tells me he lives for sex. He probably abuses the older daughters, but Vera has not yet managed to catch him at it."

I tried to be diplomatic but felt someone should defend the poor man. So, once again risking punishment, I commented.

"It must be hard for a man to live with such a dominant woman! I find it hard to be subservient to you, just consider how you would feel if you had to change places."

Fortunately, he found this hilarious, pointing out that one as great as he, never could be subservient to anybody, least of all a woman. Then reverting to the softer side of his nature. "Go on and clean yourself up, then get to bed, I'll be with you shortly."

When I crept downstairs about fifteen minutes later, he was talking to Vera on the telephone. They were laughing about Satan's attack, and I realised that she had known what to expect. Which is why she was behind him when the dog entered the room and why poor Bill was right in the line of fire. I left him to it and returned to my bed.

~~

Eventually, I gave myself a good talking to, recalling the times my husband had flirted and made himself important to other women. These occasions had grown over the mid-1970s, together with my substantial embarrassment.

However, I had ignored them, for I knew very well that they were only a necessary boost to the ego of a man who was beginning to look and feel older. He needed the attention of a younger woman…after all, I was only his wife, merely a possession. So one Friday evening, gathering my courage firmly in both hands, I informed Benedict that I would no longer act as chaperone or prepare food for them anymore. Much to my surprise, he accepted this with no argument.

~~

At the weekends, Benedict would meet his lady love, sometimes bringing her home with him. I made a point of being absent from the house every Saturday, leaving after him and returning about seven. If Vera still happened to be in the house when I arrived home, I would go straight to the bedroom and read until he took her home. But these occasions were now less frequent, as Benedict refused to bring the brat into the house without me there to supervise and entertain her.

I didn't think I could stand it much longer.

One Saturday, he gave me £100 and told me to treat myself to something nice. He drove me to Southampton and leaving me in the city centre explained that he would probably take Vera shopping in Bournemouth.

It was a chilly late October, and I was wearing flat boots, an old duffel coat and carrying two heavy bags of shopping. Suddenly, people in front of me parted and between them, hand in hand, both wearing fawn corduroy trousers and tweed jackets, appeared Benedict and Vera. With her elegant tall boots and wearing a trilby hat, she looked like a million dollars. Everyone looked at them, they couldn't help it. They, heads in the air and knowing the world was at that moment theirs, walked past me with no acknowledgement. Why should there have been, I was just another drab shopper amongst many.

Did he do that deliberately? I wondered. *Probably.* I felt diminished, humiliated and suddenly, determined to put a spoke in the wheel of this affair.

~~

Eventually, my chance came. They now took it for granted that I would not be in the house, so more frequently took to leaving the brat with her sisters. He would take Vera shopping and out to lunch, then come back to the house, confident that I would not be around. I had anticipated this move and took to remaining at home. There was no problem, as I knew Satan would warn me when his jeep drew up and I could keep out of sight.

~~

It was nearly two months before the opportunity arose, early December and a grey, cold day. I allowed the fire in the wood-burning stove to go out…actually, I'd helped it. Unfortunately, there were no firelighters, not anywhere that *he* could find anyway, and he was a man of entrenched habits.

"That damned woman has run out of firelighters," he said. "I'll just nip along to the shop and get some, okay?"

"Sure. I'll set up the chess," was her response.

I watched him cross the road and then crept quietly to free Satan. Then, checking the sitting room door was unlatched, I slipped out into the back garden and through the woods. I made my way to the village on the far side and caught a bus to the city, where I boarded the returning one.

~~

When I alighted from the seven o'clock bus with my shopping, there were still police cars around.

On his return from the shop, Ben immediately realised that the dog was loose. There was blood everywhere. Well, there would be…Satan always went for the jugular.

I was really sad when she had to be put down, which unlike with humans, is something they still do to animals that kill.

Spirits of a Different Kind

As the repeated chorus draws to its close, notes reverberate and echo through the high vaulted ceiling. Chairs scrape as those who have been standing, sit again. The voice of the pastor rings out loud and clear.

"Praise the Laard…'Allelujah…Praise the Laard." His accent changes the vowel sound.

Various voices from the congregation repeat his words, "Praise the Lord" and "Hallelujah."

"Let us pray," he says and proceeds to do so.

He then approaches a group of people sitting in the front row to his left. Raising both hands to shoulder height, palms facing outward, as if to ward off any unholy vibes, he speaks in a deep resonant voice, "Which of you has not yet received the blessing of the Laard…the blessed speaking in tongues?"

The hands of three women rise hesitantly. There are six people in the row, only one of them being a man. It can be assumed that he and the other two women *have* already received the said blessing. Those still to receive are clearly embarrassed, red of face with downcast eyes.

A plump lady in her fifties, wearing a beige coat with a small round hat of the same colour, is thinking of her deceased husband and her own loneliness.

What am I doing here? Fred would have said I'm mad. But they're a good crowd, and they've really made me feel welcome. If this is what I need to do to become one of them, then so what?

The pastor and his wife have invited her to lunch after the service and she *so* wants to conform. Cathy tries to clear her head and concentrate.

The pastor's voice drones on. "Empty your minds, clear your thoughts and think only of the Holy Spirit. Empty your heads and let him enter in."

This would be easy. Cathy finds thinking distressing these days, and her mind is frequently empty. She sits for hours in front of the television, allowing soaps and quizzes to fill the vacuum that now replaces the alert mind, which was ever present when Fred was alive. Sometimes she skims through a magazine, reading about the problems of other people. Often, she regrets her inability to have children; she could have had grandchildren to spoil by now. But there is no one. So here she is at the local Pentecostal Church. Not because she feels inclined towards their particular method of worship, but because Jenny over the road had told her that them at that church were a real comfort when her Doug passed over. Jenny doesn't go to services anymore, she has joined a ballroom dancing school and met a man, so Cathy sees little of her nowadays.

Jenny's younger than I am anyway, probably by ten years.

Cathy would have been horrified to learn that Jenny is, in fact, five years older than she is. It is just a state of mind, and Cathy's is displaying a notice that reads *vacant possession*.

From the end of the row comes a mumbling sound, and Naomi realises it is Ruth who has already received the blessing of the Holy Spirit. Naomi has only recently moved to the area. Unmarried and with no family ties. Consequently, she is the one that the large company, for which she works, chooses to move from branch to branch. She is good at her job, well thought of and well paid. Smartly dressed in a black suit with a white blouse and medium-heeled shoes. She supposes she is more or less average-looking.

Why is it I haven't managed to catch a man then? I'm slim, well thin, really.

This is not because she doesn't eat; she just doesn't put on weight. In her mid-forties, with the skin on her face starting to drop away from the bone structure, she looks sharp, uptight, and somewhat miserable. Her nose is a bit too long and her lips are thin and pursed.

I'm intelligent, aren't I? But if I hoped to find a man through this church, I can forget it.

There seems to be a distinct shortage of men and anyway, the congregation is predominantly a 'family' affair. Still, she has been invited to lunch by the pastor. You never knew, perhaps he has a son who isn't involved in this rigmarole. *Huh! Some hopes!*

Ruth's voice is in full flow now.

"*Amanio compilatim shaloma…*"

Unknown words flow from her with a booming, unnatural sound.

Rather like the voices that come through mediums at a séance, thought the third as yet unblessed woman.

The pastor is presumably translating or pretending to do so.

"Open up your hearts to the Laard and let Him enter your soul. The Holy Spirit will take up residence within you and thou shalt be blest."

Jean recalls that last week, the pastor explained how he is 'blessed to translate the tongues'. What she thinks of as 'gobbledegook'. This is obviously considered to be a great blessing and honour by the church members. Jean thinks it is more likely that certain people spouted 'gobbledegook' so that the pastor could look good. She notices there are considerably fewer words emanating from him, compared with the abundance coming forth from the mouth of Ruth.

Jean is here for one reason only. She doesn't want to get involved in this, but Andy commands and is obeyed or else! Professor Andrew Loomis PhD. MSc. is a big handsome man with deep-set dark eyes under beetle brows. Most of the people who meet him think he is just wonderful, a sentiment with which he heartily agrees. Her husband is keen to become involved in all and any form of religion, and it is automatically assumed that she will be associated with anything of interest to him. Unfortunately, when it comes to things like this, it is Jean who is compelled to indulge in the experiment. The pastor's voice penetrates her thoughts once again.

"Let your mind be open…empty your head of all thoughts but the entry of the Spirit. Relax and let him in."

With these words in her mind, Jean immediately prays.

Lord God, if it is the Holy Spirit, then please bless me, but if it is not of God, then keep me free from its influence, in the name of your Son, Christ Jesus.

She feels better after that and allows herself to think through what is happening. The thoughts spiral through her head.

Surely, if we believe in God and good, then we must believe in Satan and evil. Therefore, if the mind is open to allow an entry, how can we be sure that it is not the entry of a demon? Satan will indeed clothe himself as a lamb in order to cause chaos in the Kingdom of God.

Jean thinks she should mention this to Andy. She isn't particularly good at remembering where any special quotes might be in the Bible. It's something about a wolf in sheep's clothing, but Andy has an amazing memory for that kind of thing. She can quote more or less correctly, but he has it word for word, chapter and verse. It makes her sick. Thinking about it, she decides she doesn't like him very much. Sure, she loves him but like him? No!

Andy manages to offend most of the religious bodies with whom they come into contact. The Christian Scientists had thrown them out, as had the Mormons, the Jehovah's Witnesses, and the Spiritualists. So far as the Church of England is concerned, they haven't been chucked out yet, but the local vicar surely avoids them like the plague. Methodists, Baptists, Unitarians, and now Pentecostals. Jean doesn't think this one will last for long (too wishy-washy for Andy's taste). She wonders if he will be annoyed with her for not getting 'blessed'. On the other hand, she might go up in his estimation…not an empty vessel after all, or as green as she is cabbage-looking.

CRASH! Jean jumps. Cathy has fainted or perhaps is having a fit. She's trembling and flailing her arms about whilst apparently trying to say something in an extremely high-pitched whistling voice.

Oh God! Jean thinks, *More gobbledegook and it looks like I could be right about the wrong sort of spirit.*

The pastor stands over Cathy and prays…thanking the Laard for entering sister Cathy. Then the congregation is encouraged to get back into the repetitive choruses. Bright and tuneful enough but guaranteed to get everyone more or less brainwashed.

Cathy recovers from the faint and is helped onto a chair while people fuss around her. She revels in the attention. Obviously, something has gone right for a change. With lunch to follow, she should be the star guest. It seems this is Cathy's day.

Naomi thinks she probably dwells too much on getting a man, and too little on getting blessed.

But what the hell! Whoops! I suppose I shouldn't say things like that in a church.

On the other hand, she is somewhat relieved after seeing what happened to poor Cathy. Now, she can concentrate on lunch and if there's no hope there, then she doubts she'll bother to come here again.

The service ends and Jean glances at Andy, who glowers back at her.

Oh dear, this is going to be a bad one.

Jean knows that if Andy finds a sudden forgotten excuse not to go to the pastor's home for lunch, then she is in for a lousy few days. Until something else happens to grab the attention of her lord and – expert of whatever is his interest of the moment – master.

Lord and master be damned! she thinks.

Then feels guilty for thinking such thoughts in a church. Perhaps he'll still join the luncheon party, in which case, all will probably be fine again.

She wonders when Andy's evil spirit entered him and thinks it was probably during his childhood. It's a clever thing that spirit, remaining hidden for most of the time, and never appearing in public, then *WHAM!* There it is, and Jean, being the only one around, is caught. No, she is glad things have turned out this way. Good and evil are inevitabilities in the world, and Jean thinks it is down to each person to fill their lives with one or the other. But for sure, there's no way *she* is going to create an empty vessel to be filled!

Filial Differences

"I hate him!

He's not beautiful. He's a funny little object. God is cruel. I wouldn't have minded a sister, but that *thing* is a boy. And he can't have his birthday the day after mine. I won't share it with him. I don't want him, please, Nanny, send him back."

The little girl buried her head in her grandmother's lap and sobbed with rage and disappointment. There was no doubt she did not like the new baby. At seven years and one day old, this darling granddaughter had received the entire devotion of her parents and grandparents.

The grandmother thought, *We've loved this child too much, spoilt her by making her the centre of our lives, but she's such a bright child.*
She smiled as she remembered the little girl when she was three, recovering from mumps, tucked up on the sofa. She'd given Kate a Mabel Lucy Atwell storybook, containing a number of stories, with large print and illustrations. When she returned to the room, Kate had said, "Listen, Nanny, I'll read you this story."

She'd thought Kate was telling the story through the pictures until, looking over the child's shoulder, she realised that this infant could truly read.

Richard was born in a nursing home on the Isle of Wight. Her mother had been there for Kate's birthday, and the baby was born late the next day, but Kate didn't mind her mother not being around, as long as Nanny was in charge of her young life.

She had been enrolled at the village school, which she loved. On the mainland, she attended a large school with hundreds of pupils, but here, the church school accommodated less than one hundred.

The ages in Kate's class ranged from five to seven, and they were grouped according to ability. It was obvious from the beginning that Kate would be in the top group for reading and she was determined to do well in all subjects. Sums were different, Kate struggled, but she tackled the problem with enthusiasm.

During morning break, the children were allowed to leave the playground, to go to the bakery next door. What they bought was a sticky current bun, costing one penny. Oh, the delightful smell of hot bread and buns! The sticky fingers and exhalations of sweet cloudy breath, as mouths were mildly burnt by the hot delicious buns. This was a school in which Kate felt comfortable and she wished Mummy and Daddy would move here.

Then she remembered her new brother. Nothing would ever be the same again. Mummy had a baby to look after, and *'it'* seemed to need an awful lot of attention. Kate stayed at the church school for the whole term, while Mummy took the new baby back to the mainland.

"You'll have such fun playing with your little brother. Think how you'll be able to teach him to read like you. Richard will love his big sister." Nanny tried to encourage some enthusiasm in the child for her new brother but Kate would have none of it.

"I won't have anything to do with him. I hate him," she said.

By the time her mother and the baby returned to the Island for the last two weeks of term, during which the baby was christened, the grandmother thought she had more or less talked Kate into accepting her new brother. However, when people admired the baby saying, "Aren't you lucky to have such a beautiful brother?" Kate would reply, "He's a funny little object and I don't like him."

"Don't worry," the people said quietly to her mother, "she's just jealous…that's natural but she will soon grow to love him."

Kate's mother hoped so, but as time passed, there was no sign of acceptance.

As the little boy grew and was old enough to play, he rode the tricycle, of which Kate had taken such care since she was three. It was soon scratched and having been left out in the rain a few times, was rusting. He ran her doll's pram into the wall, tearing the hood and scratching the paintwork.

One day, when he was whinging that he was bored and Kate was curled up in a corner with a book, her mother told her to let Richard play with her dresser and miniature Goss-China tea set. It was old, valuable white bone Goss-China, with a gold rim and green pattern around the edges, comprising a full matching set of twelve each, dinner and tea sets, with a teapot, milk jug and sugar basin to match. Kate's father had made the dresser. It took Richard less than half an hour to break the teapot, two cups and four plates. The irreplaceable set was ruined, and Kate was heartbroken.

~~

More time passed, and Richard started school. Aged ten, Kate had passed a scholarship to a small private school that suited her very well. It was in a big old house; the classes were small and the tuition excellent.

When she was fourteen, her beloved grandmother died, followed within eighteen months by her grandfather, finally severing Kate's contact with the Island.

Her brother was now almost as tall as Kate but showed no indication of being as bright as his sister, and whereas Kate could read at the age of three, Richard was nearly nine before he could do so. He showed no inclination to actually do anything at all. His father moved him to another school where he did a little better than previously, but it was obvious he wasn't going anywhere.

Kate eventually qualified as a journalist and joined a local paper, but before her brother was old enough to leave school, she moved to a large London paper. She travelled abroad in connection with her job, and although she kept in touch with her parents by letter, she rarely visited her old home and made no contact with her brother.

~~

Their parents split up and Richard effectively lived off both of them for several years. Eventually, he met and married an Irish girl. Rita could neither read nor write, but she could keep house and was an excellent cook. Richard went from job to job, never staying for long, though whether by choice or necessity was not clear. He and Rita produced two children and looked to his mother, who was remarried to a wealthy man, to get them out of debt. At one point, they decided to emigrate, then for some reason, this fell through. Another flat was rented, furnished and carpeted once again by Richard's mother.

Shortly after this, Richard and Kate's father died, and the siblings met once again. They tried, for the sake of their mother, to be friendly, but there was no affection whatsoever between them. This was mainly due to the fact that Kate had a good, well-remunerated career, and drove a new car, whereas Richard was still 'jobbing' around and couldn't even drive. Later, he did learn to do so and borrowed money from his mother to buy a second-hand car.

The jealousy Kate had felt as a child had long ago resolved into indifference. She just got on with life and spared not a thought for her brother or his family.

~~

Then her mother's husband died, and Kate moved back into the area, so that she could support her mother as necessary. She still travelled abroad frequently but with a small cottage in the New Forest, was able to visit her mother daily whenever she *was* home.

One day, her mother telephoned to ask if Richard's daughter could borrow Kate's crystals for her wedding.

Kate said, "That's fine, I'll bring them with me when I come over there next."

The following day, a call from her mother was almost impossible to understand. The old lady was sobbing and trying to talk at the same time.

"Mum! Please calm down, dear, what's the matter? I'm on my way now, okay?"

Leaving her lunch, Kate locked up and drove post-haste to her mother's house. By the time she got there, the old lady had calmed down somewhat and was able to explain the cause of her distress.

"Richard and Rita came in this morning. I said I would make some coffee, but they didn't want any, said they just wanted to talk to me. I wondered what the matter was. Thought he probably wanted some more money. I'd only given him a hundred and sixty pounds last week for a freezer. So I said, well sit down anyway. But Richard said they didn't want to sit, they would stand. I'd sat down by then. I was feeling a bit shaky I can tell you."

She brushed a tear from her cheek, drew a resolute breath and continued.

"Then he started on me. He said I'd no right to give you the crystals because I'd promised all my jewellery to Rita. I'd given her my round watch. I kept the little gold one for you, dear. He went on and on about how you had everything. A good education and job. And your own house. He said, why hadn't he had a private education and surely a boy's more important than a girl is. He's just jealous because you've done so well."

"But Mum," Kate interrupted, "I won a scholarship to that school, and I got my job through hard work. Richard couldn't have passed a scholarship to save his life, he was always lazy and stupid…Sorry, Mum, I shouldn't have said that."

"Why not, dear? It's true I'm afraid and it's my fault. I always did get him out of trouble, paid his debts and furnished his house…twice. I even gave him five thousand pounds for that car. That was supposed to be a loan, but I haven't seen any signs of it being paid back yet."

The old lady sniffed and wiped her already red eyes.

Kate stood. "I'm going to make some tea, Mum. Come on, let's go into the kitchen and you can tell me more as I make it."

She sat her mother down at the kitchen table and filled the kettle.

"He said I should leave him the house. Rita kept saying I'd promised to give her all my jewellery, and in the end, I got really cross. I told her she was an ignorant bog-arab and should be grateful that I'd got them out of debt so often. I told them straight that they were council house types and deserved no more than they had. Then I said that after today, I would consider changing my Will so they didn't even get half the house. Rita swore at me and came at me with her hand raised. I thought she would hit me, but Richard grabbed her and dragged her, still screaming abuse at me, out the door…then I phoned you."

She gave a shuddering sob and putting her head in her hands, cried as though her heart would break. Kate gathered her mother in her arms and the two women cried together, for the very sadness of filial differences.

Later, having packed a small case, Kate drove her mother back to the New Forest for a few days.

When December came, the old lady decided to try and break what was now a six-month silence and sent a Christmas card to her son. Kate again received a tearful telephone call and hastened to her mother's side.

The card had been returned, unopened. Written across the top of the envelope were the words, '*NOT WANTED AT THIS ADDRESS*'. The old lady now knew that she had irrevocably lost her son and wished with all her heart that she had never borne more than one child.

Kate restrained her mother from altering her Will for as long as she could. She explained that she would rather know nothing about it, as it was unethical. In the end, her mother telephoned a solicitor friend and arranged for him to call on her privately, at home. Thus, the deed was done.

When the old lady died in her nineties, her estranged son remained that way, not deigning to attend the funeral.

And Kate? She just got on with her life as usual; a loner with an interesting career, gained by her own endeavours.

If anyone asks if she has any brothers or sisters, she says, "No!"

Doctor Darkwater

Miles FitzLucan – Part I

Miles FitzLucan cursed as he lay on his bed in pain.

He had once been a handsome man, with broad shoulders and legs like tree trunks. In the communal showers after a game of rugby, the guys referred to him as 'kangaroo balls'. There was no doubt that with his six-foot height, head of thick hair and film star looks, he could pull any girl he wanted.

Now here he was, either with the use of the sharp intellect that had always prevailed or having taken painkillers, drugged to a state of near senility. The trouble was, with his brain functioning, the pain was almost unbearable.

When he thought back, the disease had probably been creeping up on him over the last ten years, but he'd ignored the twinges, as just that. Nothing could hurt him. But the disease had suddenly flared up. His joints swelled, but the medication brought him up in blisters. It was changed and they went down again. The pain flared up again. More medication and these worked. He felt better and stopped taking the tablets. He was pain-free and nearly back to normal for five whole days, then it was back again with a vengeance. The disease developed at an incredible number of knots, and after only six months, he was obliged to take to a wheelchair. Now, a year later, he was practically bedridden.

He needed a permanent nurse!

He had a permanent nurse!

He was married to a bloody nurse!

"Damn it! Damn her to hell! Oh God, what have I done?"

Miles had heard it said that when struck by sudden death, your life flashes before your eyes. He knew he was indeed marked by death but thought he had time. No quick release for him. It could be six months, six weeks, or if he was lucky, six days.

He shouted.

"Helena Rose, bring me my cassette recorder. Come on, woman, hurry!"

He must get the gist of his story down. Had to try and get it to Suzanne.

His nurse/wife quietly entered the room, a small recorder in her hand. She was nearly as tall as Miles, ten years younger than his first wife and the antithesis of Suzanne, whom he now realised that although older, was nevertheless, small, rounded and pretty. Helena Rose was not by any means unattractive, with her short blond hair and large breasts. These were what had first attracted Miles to her. Suzanne had only small hillocks and tiny soft nipples. Those of Helena Rose were a double D-cup, her nipples large and erect, with legs that seemed to go on forever, her shoulders broad and square. Whereas little Suzanne had a plump soft posterior, his second wife had an almost masculine bottom.

What have I done? I hate this woman and she hates me.

"Give it here then. Well, what are you waiting for? Have you got nothing to do? Get out."

"Can you manage the recorder, Mi?" Helena Rose asked quietly as she retreated to the door.

He hated the abbreviation of his name. Didn't allow such shortening of any name, and she knew it. If looks could indeed kill, he would have relieved himself of her irritating presence right then before she left the room, but Miles knew he could not manage without her.

Pressing the two buttons simultaneously to record was difficult, his fingers had no strength and the pain that shot through them was excruciating. He tried again, swore, and exasperated, tried to relax against his pillows, squeezing his eyes tightly shut. Unexpected tears rolled down his sunken cheeks, resting in the creases until they dried like crusted, sun-baked rivulets. He would try again later.

Then his life as it had been in 1953 began to unravel before his eyes, not unlike watching the man he once was, performing in a film.

~~

Dr Darkwater will be furious. I was late last week.

Miles FitzLucan broke into a run. He'd had trouble crossing the busy main road and his appointment with the psychiatrist was at two-thirty. Five minutes, perhaps he could make it.

Dr Darkwater was a tall thin man of gangling aspect. He was invariably dressed in a black shirt with blood red tie and a black suit, the matching leather shoes shining so brightly that they reflected. His hair was also black, smooth against his head from a peak low on his forehead. Miles shuddered involuntarily; he reminded him of Count Dracula. He realised that what he felt about this man was fear and wondered how such a character came to be such a big name in his field.

"Ah, Miles!"

His mellifluous voice flows over me. It's like being wrapped in a soft mohair blanket and I relax into the large soft armchair that is his preference over the usual couch.

"You have been running, relax and catch your breath. Count slowly…one…two…three…"

I count to myself and feel my heartbeat slow down and my breath becomes even. I feel safe now.

"You are ten years old, it is night-time, dark. Where are you, Miles?"
I answer in my tearful ten-year-old boy voice, *"I'm in bed. They're going to put me in a children's home for being naughty."*
"What did you do?"

"I ambushed Rick Chambers in the cemetery. I tied him up and pushed him down a freshly dug grave, then threw leaves on top of him. It was only a game. Rick's a coward. He screamed and yelled 'til someone found him. I was going to get him out later."

"But you didn't, Miles, did you? Poor Rick was in that new grave for over an hour."
I giggled.

"Yeah, I forgot him. I was playing football, then it was teatime. Then his dad came round and told on me. She yelled at me and said I had to go straight to bed, and they'd think about whether to put me in a home for bad boys."

I remembered how scared I'd been, how I curled up under the blankets in the dark…I thought about it. Then Darkwater spoke, bringing me back in line.

"Miles? Tell me what happened then."

"She was going to pour boiling oil in my eyes. I'm scared to go to sleep in case I miss her creeping in."

I was scared, shivering with apprehension.

"Who are you afraid of, Miles?"

"Her. My mother! She hates me. She wants to blind me so I'll have to be good, because I can't see to do bad things.

"Relax Miles, you are safe. In future when you hear my voice in your head, you will telephone the number on the card I shall give you as you leave today. I shall count and when I reach three, you will wake up. You will feel refreshed and will not remember what we have discussed. One…two…three."

~~

I was so comfortable in this armchair. I stretched my arms above my head and asked him what great insight he could offer me for my problem.

"I would suggest that you find yourself a good wife, who will take care of your needs and with whom you can set up a home of your own. You will then be in control of your own domain, and I suspect life will become more pleasant for you."

I liked that.

"Should I see you again, Doctor Darkwater?" I asked.

"I think if you take my advice, you will not find that necessary. Meanwhile, here is an exemption form, which you should return to the appropriate National Service office. I have signed it, as I feel you are unsuited to military service."

"Thank you, sir."

I picked up the precious piece of paper, shook his hand, and left his office for the last time.

Safely outside and round the corner out of sight, I jumped high, punching the air. I had achieved what I wanted. What a clever fellow I am…what an actor. I had been attending consultations with Dracula for the past six weeks. Fancy the stupid little man thinking he could hypnotise *me*! In just three weeks, I would graduate. I was almost a Bachelor of Science. Naturally, I would achieve my degree. The trouble was that my deferment of military service was also at an end, and I would be expected to go into the army for two years. I did not want this, hence my mental problems. Good, eh! But I liked his idea of having a home of my own, with a little wifie to run it and look after yours truly. A life controlled entirely by me. It was time to start collecting the necessary chattels.

~~

Of course, at that time I didn't have his notes. I was not aware that Doctor Darkwater *had* in fact hypnotised me…

Have I ever heard his voice…telephoned him?

I do not know…

Searching for Someone Suitable

Miles FitzLucan – Part II

Dr Darkwater had put in my mind, a suggestion that I would best get full control of my own life by getting married. So I put together a list of potential possibilities and contacted each one in turn, starting with…

Wendy: She was a few years younger than yours truly, was still at the convent and had just sat her exams for university. I had known her since I was fifteen. I always found convent girls very willing, even anxious for experience of sex. Probably because of the all-female environment, and a natural desire to rebel against the establishment.

Subversive rebellion, which was the way I had always reacted at St Patrick's, a boy's only school, run by Jesuits. Hell! I wasn't even a Catholic. Anyway, with my photographic memory, I'd never needed to bother much with homework, just half an hour to scribble it down in time for the ritualistic homework hour with Father Franklyn. Which left me with time to spare for the all-important sexual experience. But I digress.

However, Wendy had always proved strongly against it, where seduction was concerned. Now I was going to try not only to seduce her but also to dissuade her from going to university, where she intended to study law and to marry me instead.

Wearing grey slacks with a cream turtleneck shirt and a blazer, I turned up at the pre-arranged meeting place only twenty minutes late. Another of my little ploys. I find that a girl will often hang around for nearly an hour before giving up.

I kept a girl waiting outside the cinema one night and watched her. She walked up and down, periodically peering around the corner just in case she was in the wrong place after all. When only five minutes short of the hour, she gave a final look at her wristwatch and as she turned to walk away, I called her name.

She looked about to bawl me out, so I jumped in quickly. "You're early, it's only five to. Have you been waiting long?" That, of course, immediately cooled the situation as she was no longer sure whether we had arranged to meet at six or seven o'clock.

Anyway, Wendy was waiting for me, looking just the sort of girl I could comfortably take home to meet my mother. Clothes would be one of the first things I would take in hand. She was wearing expensive casual dark green shoes matching her warm green coat that was crimped in at the waist, with a high deep collar pulled up to protect her from the wind. Later, I saw that she wore a grey skirt that came below her knees and a polo-neck sweater, again in her favourite dark green. I visualised her in a full shocking-pink skirt with an extremely low-cut black top, something off the shoulders, possibly trimmed with fur, worn with really high black stilettos. Mmmm! Just thinking about it turns me on.

I had splashed out for the evening by taking her to a rather nice restaurant. She could have dressed up a bit, you'd think. We ordered our food, and I did the impressive bit with the wine tasting. Can't think why…they open a brand new bottle and then give the punters a chance to critique the contents…a load of rubbish, in my opinion, but it goes down well with the fillies.

Wendy made one glass of wine last all evening and wouldn't accept a top-up. I tried to break the ice by talking about university, which was when I came to the full understanding that she was not under any circumstances, a suitable wifie for yours truly.

I asked, "Do you really want to go to university for all those years of study? What if you wanted to get married?"

She actually laughed, as though I'd made a joke.

"If I should, at some time in the future, decide to marry, it will have to fit around my career as a barrister. To get there is going to take me at least ten years. Anyway, why on earth should I want to be saddled with a man who would probably be under the misapprehension that I was there for his convenience? No way Jose!"

That confirmed my thoughts, and I certainly wasn't going to get lucky tonight. Now, I had to fix up another date with another girl…damn it! This could be expensive.

~~

Celia: was my next choice. She was from the same background as Wendy, so far as education was concerned, and about the same age. However, all similarities ended there. Celia preferred to be called Cee and was a keen sportswoman. She rode a boy's racing bike, with drop handlebars, played tennis for her school and was in the county team. She also swam competitively, was short-listed for the Olympic relay race team, skated, and played ice hockey in the season. Generally an all-rounder. Oh! I nearly forgot, Celia also rode horseback and indulged in fox hunting (Daddy was Master of the Hunt). He was a straight-backed, boring old fart if ever there was one.

Anyway, Celia was definitely one of the crowd, a good sort, known amongst us chaps as the 'Hunt Bicycle'.

My date with Celia was to be a trip to the theatre. Personally, I loathe musicals, but I knew through the grapevine that she was mad about them and something or other big from America, complete with a star cast, was coming to the theatre in town. So I got a friend who was going into town that day, to book and pay for a couple of tickets. Then I phoned her to arrange things. The tickets were to be held for FitzLucan at the kiosk, and by the time I arrived, they had already been picked up.

"The gentleman said two seats in the circle had been reserved in the name of FitzLucan, sir. He and the young lady went right up about fifteen minutes ago."

That was that. The bitch used the tickets I had paid for and left me standing like a lemon. The only reason I'd arranged to pick them up from the ticket office was because I would not be seeing my *friend* for a couple of days.

Celia had the cheek to phone me the next day, to thank me for treating her and Hugh. I nearly burst at that...he was the bastard who booked them.

I did, of course, learn from that experience by acknowledging that I had no friends, only acquaintances according to their usefulness. Still abide by it to this day.

They got engaged the following month, but I didn't get an invitation to the party. Wouldn't have gone, anyway.

They never did get married though. Hugh had a crash in his MG sports car shortly after the engagement. The papers reported that someone had cut partly through the brake cable. He always did drive erratically, anyway.

Celia was supposed to have been with him. They were going to Wimbledon to watch the finals. Unfortunately, she had food poisoning, so the obnoxious Hugh died alone.

Perhaps I should brush up on toxins. Too late for Celia *now though.*

I should have had that car…I should have had Celia and all her money. Whatever! I must now think about someone else to be my chattel.

~~

Georgina: was next on my list. She was a bit older than me but as far as I knew was still unattached and already had her MSc. One very clever lady was Georgina, probably on a par with myself, which made her a formidable companion. She was very into smart dressy clothes, worn with three-inch stilettos, which I like! Only slightly shorter than me, she was tall for a woman. Her figure was surprisingly good, even though she lacked much in the boob department. Perhaps her shoulders were a little wide but it was difficult to tell because she liked to wear smart suits with shoulder pads and shirt blouses, which she sometimes wore with a tie. However, she had long legs, and I could at least be sure that her calves and ankles were pretty neat. With luck, I should be in a position to judge the rest later.

I decided to wine and dine her and also to arrive on time. The cow kept *me* waiting for half an hour and I found it exceedingly difficult to produce my lady-killer smile. Anyway, it proved to be a very enjoyable evening. We had much in common, both intellectually and professionally. We loved opera, hated golf, and enjoyed good food. I also soon learnt that she abhorred the fuss with wine tasting, so I just told the waiter to stick the bottle on the table and we would drink it. We did too, and another one as well, plus brandy with our coffee.

Later, I walked her home and was invited in for a drink. That was another surprise. I was not aware that she had her own flat. It was large and comfortable, apparently furnished by devoted parents as a reward for graduating with honours.

We listened to various opera highlights and enthusiastically discussed the orchestras, the conductors, and the singers, whilst imbibing a very passable Irish whiskey. Georgina obviously liked her liquor and was able to hold it well. However, alcohol does tend to loosen the tongue, and I was about to learn why she was also unsuited to be my wife.

She had just informed me that she preferred to be called George when I heard a key turning in the front door. Georgina jumped up and flung herself into the arms of the person who entered the room. They hugged and kissed for a while, and then, looking very flushed and pretty, Georgina found time to introduce her friend to me.

"This is Victoria," she said. "Vicky is a doctor and she's just finished a twenty-hour stint at the Royal."

We shook hands. God, she was gorgeous. Even wearing flat shoes, I could tell her legs were good. She had what I can only describe as 'a jolly derrière', a narrow waist and the sort of bust I would like to bury my head between.

"It's good of you to entertain George for me. She gets pretty lonely when I'm on duty. Thank you."

She even possessed a sexy voice!

I guess I must have given some suitable reply, but I can't remember what it was, and soon after took my leave of them. Bloody dikes! That was another one down the drain.

~~

Somewhere in between the ensuing eighteen months, I had found employment with a chemical research company, which with my qualifications and magnificent demeanour, was comparatively easy. I was given a small laboratory all to myself, where I could work on special projects. Impressive, eh! Anyway, that was where I got myself some interesting experiences with the girl who delivered the mail and ran messages.

~~

Sharon: was petite, without the expected impressions *I* receive from that word, of one who is a small dainty person of quality. Whilst she was undoubtedly small and dainty, with a mass of blond curls bouncing around an elfin face, she was just about as common as you can get. She wore her mini-skirts just that little bit shorter than other women and her tops a little more revealing of her perfectly rounded breasts. The high slender heels of her shoes were bright red, adhering to narrow feet by means of thin red straps, fastened above shapely ankles with buckled straps.

She looked a dream…provided she kept her mouth shut. That voice! It was the typical rasp of a smoker, but not simply hard…it was loud. I mean LOUD! It was coarse too, every 'H' hitting the ground before it could possibly be enunciated, every 'T' clipped and wherever able, the 'th' sound was also dropped. But the vocal sounds emitting from those delightful kissable lips, were not the only discrepancy of that body part, for Sharon did not chew, she chomped at her food, sounding like a pig at the trough. More unfortunate, she perpetually chewed gum.

The small laboratory I named *The Hovel*, that sign replacing the one carrying my name, sported a loft, which I found I could reach by standing on a lab stool and pulling myself upwards. The muscles in my arms, of course, were incredibly strong. I had acquired a straw bail and spread it over the boards to form a place to lay Sharon, who was ready, willing, and extremely able.

I shall never know where she got such colossal sexual experience. Surely, it could not be doing what came naturally, although natural is certainly the way it seemed. I enjoyed these experiences nearly every weekday for all the time I worked at the research centre, right up to that day the bastards decided to dispense with my presence.

She was quite something. I soon banned chewing gum and prevented her from talking by keeping my lips firmly pressed against hers. However, there was no way I could take her as a wife…so I must proceed with my search.

I finally found my Miss Right whilst still consorting regularly with Sharon.

~~

Suzanne: was small, petite even, almost pretty with thick dark shining hair, flowing down to her waist. Her eyes were dark brown that gazed at yours truly with the adoration of a Newfoundland puppy. She could dance too, which is where I first discovered her and carefully pursued her for more than a year. I needed to do that, although it went against the grain for me, because she was only sixteen years old and was still at school. I was at that time, seven years older than Suzanne, and knew for a fact that she was a totally virginal innocent.

Her father regularly functioned as master of ceremonies for the monthly dance at a local ballroom. These affairs were not bad and were a good place to find unattached women, of whom there were usually at least half a dozen who regularly danced together, for lack of male partners. Dress at these dances was optional, but I decided to go clothed. *Sorry, my ready wit still breaks loose occasionally.* Suzanne's parents invariably wore full evening dress, but she was usually dressed like a little kid in her Sunday best.

I, of course, always arrived late. My timing was actually impeccable, just in time to ask Suzanne for the dance prior to a break for refreshments. I would then take her with me to purchase disgusting coffee and a cake, returning to my seat at the edge of the ballroom, as far away from the fond parents as possible. She remained with me for the rest of the evening, during which I learned what I could and plied her with charm. During the last waltz, I left her at her parent's table before the end, grabbed my outdoor shoes and was on my way home before it finished. That is always a good ploy, making her wonder if she would see me next month and her parents trying to turn her against me. They never did like me, didn't understand me, of course. After all, they were pretty boring, normal people.

Suzanne took my advice, of course, and duly left her private school without sitting the exams that would have undoubtedly got her a university place. As it was, she obtained a post with a firm of solicitors, which served to expand her non-existent knowledge as to how the other half lived.

I spent two years breaking her in, at the end of which she was my obedient slave, not daring to cross me for fear of losing her handsome boyfriend. I introduced her to my penis, of which she seemed to be terrified.

This was when I realised for the first time that Suzanne had no knowledge whatsoever of the differences between the bodies of men and women, let alone sex. So it was that it became necessary for me to explain to her the facts of life. Poor kid, but I promised not to make the male/female engagement until such time as we might be married. However, I did make it quite clear that I expected petting, to quite a considerable degree, to which she agreed on the grounds that if she loved me, she would naturally be prepared to 'go nearly all the way'.

Things got more interesting from that point. We would spend the whole of a Sunday together, having told her mother that we were meeting friends to go to various places. In fact, we mostly found ourselves a quiet secluded spot and settled down for the rest of the day with a picnic, flasks of coffee and bottles of fizzy drink. Sometimes, we would build a hide with bent branches covered with ferns and the like. In very chilly weather, we burrowed into the hay in a barn attached to the farm of one farmer or another. I often wonder what one of them thought, when he discovered the bright red and green skirt that somehow got lost amongst his hay. That night, she had to arrive home at a time when her parents were not likely to open the front door. Her legs must have been frozen, bare as they were.

It was alongside the lake in the grounds of a large estate attached to a mansion, that I took her virginity. No, I kept my word…always do. She fussed a bit but was soon brought under control and although I don't think she got much out of the experience, I very much enjoyed the whole operation. I recall considering the next step…Hmmm.

I clearly remember the first occasion I was obliged to inflict physical punishment on her. I had made a flask of coffee, to which I had added copious amounts of sugar, because that is the way I like it, although I knew full well that Suzanne couldn't stand sweet drinks. She took a sip, said "Ugh" and threw the precious brew to the ground. I removed my belt, put her over my knees, and thwacked her soundly. She, of course, blubbered, whereupon I drew her tenderly to me and explained her foolishness. She promised never again to be so wicked, and all was forgiven. I believe in instant punishment, followed by the offender's repentance and my gracious forgiveness.

Anyway, I decided we should be married and being a gentleman, I bought her an engagement ring and went to tell her parents the great news. It is hard to imagine, but her father had the temerity to tell me he was not happy to see his daughter marrying me. What on earth did he expect for her…a bloody duke? He seemed not to appreciate the great honour I was doing his miserable family, by allowing a union between it and the superior FitzLucans. So I told him straight.

"If you refuse to willingly allow us to marry, I will make sure your daughter is pregnant, then you will be only too pleased to give us your blessing."

The stupid little twerp said, "I do not like you, Miles. You are rude and inordinately arrogant. However, if Suzanne still wishes to marry you in one year's time, when she is nineteen, then I will not stand in your way."

And that's the way it was.

Then it was time for her to meet my parents. Suzanne and my mother tolerated each other in a polite manner but my father adored her. He had nicknames for everyone, mine being Mackerel. No, I have no idea why, but Suzanne became Sprat Marigold. It takes a sprat to catch a mackerel. Boom! Boom!

We were married and one year later, I was banished from the research centre. I must say that Suzanne was completely supportive and got herself a job to support the pair of us, while I kept looking for suitable employment. That took nearly another year and all that time we said nothing of the situation to our families, despite the difficulties.

I cannot say ours was a happy marriage, but so far as the rest of humanity was concerned, it was ideal, as neither of us had the inclination to wash our dirty linen in public.

This state lasted until I met someone else, some twenty-five years later.

I have always had my hobbies, such as model railways, which Suzanne always followed along, if not willingly, then without any argument. She typed letters to other enthusiasts for me, made models and produced rubber moulds manufactured from coal for mountains. Tagging along as she had done throughout our marriage, knowing that to do so kept the peace, kept me happy, which, after all, was always of paramount importance.

I invariably regretted it after the necessity of punishing her, but I was always most careful to make sure punches were aimed at her soft breasts or somewhere on the body where bruises could not be seen.

~~

It was Citizens Band Radio that did it. The first and only thing that Suzanne flatly refused in which to become involved. At the time it started its popularity, the radio band was illegal, which of course, is what drew me to it in the first place. Helena Rose was one of the people to whom I spoke. One evening, I recall clearly that the atmosphere was charismatic, and I felt a pleasant sensation sweep through my body. This woman was magical. From that time, we spoke together most evenings, until eventually a meeting was arranged. I ordered Suzanne to accompany me, and she dared to voice her feelings about the visit and her opinion of the exciting woman that she'd never even spoken to. Very unwise! It ensured her future as 'chaperone' to my new ladylove. New, but not the first by a long chalk. I had mostly kept all my alliances safely from Suzanne and it was not until I became involved with CB radio that I decided it would be fun to openly include her. I would take her to dances or parties and flirt outrageously with other women. On more than one occasion, I recall fondling another woman in front of Suzanne, and suggesting she joined us too. This period was not much fun though as she would sit quietly until I indicated that it was time to go home, then in her maddening manner, she would wish our host goodbye and retreat to the car. So I tended to back off this game until I met Helena Rose and fell hopelessly in lust with her.

Helena Rose had, at some time between the birthing of her numerous daughters, found time to study psychology. She was rather good and combined with my own particular turn of mind, we made a formidable team. What we did to Suzanne, both psychologically and physically, was amazing. It got so she knew at some point she would have to be removed from my life one way or another, and that scared her, which was the object of the exercise. That was when I learnt my wife had more to her than I had thought possible. By this time Suzanne was working as a reporter for a local newspaper, and one weekend at the beginning of March she blithely informed me, "I've bought myself a house and will be moving on the 23rd of this month. Do close your mouth, Miles, you look foolish."

The bitch had gone behind my back and bought a bloody house. But that was not all…

"I shall need you to help me move…you, not her. I also require a divorce. It's up to you how you manage it. We can do it the easy way, irreconcilable behaviour on your part, after a friendly separation of two years, or I can drag you and her through the mill of adultery, fornication, and the rest."

"Don't be ridiculous," I told her. "I would have you on your knees in very short order."

That was when she told me how, over the past six months, she had secretly made recordings of our conversations. Not only those though, but she had also actually recorded Helena Rose and me during our 'games' with her. These she had apparently duplicated, one copy having been given to her doctor, the other enclosed in an envelope addressed to a solicitor friend. This was apparently locked in her desk at work with instructions that it should be passed to him, should she meet an untimely death or inexplicably disappear.

Game set and match to Suzanne.

The Janitor

Li'l Bastids! But beautiful!

This thought silenced his anger.

I know they giggle an' makes faces be'ind me back. Just 'cos I'm the janitor. If I was a bloody teacher, they'd have a deal more respect.

He flexes his muscles and gives a leonine growl.

I'm one han'some sum'v a bitch.

He preens before the mirror.

All the birds fancy me!

He is a little less than six feet tall with the muscular body of a regular exerciser, a firm square jaw and dark wavy hair. Only the eyes, cold ice blue, give pause for thought.

"Hello, Jace."

The voice is husky, sexy, wanting. The speaker is older than Jace by some ten years, but Ami is still a very good-looking woman. Her eyes are cat green and her hair golden red, an Irish beauty with long shapely legs and a busty figure.

"What're you doin' here this time-a day? Shouldn't you be teachin' the little darlin's to add up two an' two?"

"Don't be sarcastic, darling. I thought we could inspect the boilers, while the headmaster gives everyone a talk on how to avoid being murdered on the way home. Since that girl from my form disappeared last Saturday, everyone's running around like a headless chicken." She giggled. "Except for the headmaster, of course."

Ami is a shallow woman with no real vocation for the teaching post she holds. She is more interested in her own sexual requirements than the disappearance of one of her pupils, and at the present time, Jason Higgs is able to fulfil these, although he is unaware of the fact that she feels no affection for him whatsoever.

"Have the Pigs got any leads on that one yet?"

"No. Not a single clue, so far as they are letting on, but I guess they'll get around to questioning everyone here before long. I expect they'll be asking people to provide DNA samples too. Anyway, forget that stuff and let's have." She glances at her watch. "Fifteen minutes' exercise. Come on, Jace, what the hell's the matter with you? You're usually panting for it."

"Sure I'm pantin', love, but not right now, I'll see you later. I'm expectin' a delivery an' if I'm not 'ere to receive it, the man'll just take it away again, then your headmaster'll have my balls."

Ami pouts and glancing around to make sure they are not overlooked, kisses him, long, with a probing tongue. Then, with a wriggle of her rounded posterior, returns towards the school buildings.

Jace watches until she is far away, then enters the boiler room. It is warm in there, and he wipes the back of his hand across a perspiring forehead as he walks to the far corner, where there is a walk-in storage cupboard.

～～

Jace had discovered the secret room accidentally, shortly after he started his appointment. He was sorting through the cupboard and brushing away cobwebs when suddenly, the panel opened. On shining a torch under the shelf, he discovered a button that had been accidentally pressed by his broom. There were six steps leading down. Jace fetched a torch, which revealed a room of roughly three metres square. It was dirty, smelled foul and had apparently served at some time, as an enclosure to a main sewer entrance. Realising its advantages, Jace gradually adapted the room to suit his multifarious intentions.

～～

He unlocks the cupboard door and reaches for the button, hidden by an assortment of paint tins. A panel at the rear slides open, revealing a bare bulb, set in the ceiling under a metal grill. There is a single metal-framed bed with a mattress and quilt against the far wall. A table stands on a threadbare rug in the centre of the floor, with a single worn wooden chair. On the table are a plastic cup, some food, and crumpled food wrappings. A sink is fixed to one wall over which is suspended an old brass tap. Jace's gaze rests first on the bed and its unfortunate inhabitant.

A girl of about thirteen is curled up on the mattress, wrapped in the quilt.

Emma Fawn is an incredibly beautiful girl, intelligent and determined to become a zoo vet. But now her light blond hair is matted and looking considerably darker than its natural colour. Violet eyes are red and swollen from too much crying and too little sleep. Her English rose complexion is completely hidden by bruises and grime, rubbed in with tears.

Emma whimpers and cowers into the corner as she watches her captor enter, closing the panel behind him. One leg is chained to the frame of the bed, the chain long enough to allow her to reach the sink for water and the bucket beneath. No attempt has been made to gag her, as even if someone enters the boiler room, no sound from her prison can escape.

She knows what to expect now, having been imprisoned since last Friday. Six days now…six scratches on the brick behind the bed. Each morning, he brings her food that is supposed to last throughout the day. Crisps, fruit, biscuits, cheese and once ham and salad sandwiches, never anything hot, and she yearns for burgers and chips. Early morning is food time, and he has already left today's supply. Any other visits are when he pulls the quilt from her naked body and forces himself into her. She has learnt not to try and fight him, or the beatings that accompany the rapes will be even more painful.

"It'll be a week tomorrow, Emm dear."

That dreaded voice. How could someone who looks like God's gift to women be so evil? She'd tried to talk to him on the second day, almost succeeded but he'd suddenly slapped her face, flat of hand one side, knuckles the other. That seemed to excite him, the rape was harder and it was the first time he used the bottle. Since then, she never knows exactly what to expect, apart from pain. Today, he carries a rifle.

Emma shudders, chilled by more than cold, gripped by the fear that today will indeed be her last.

"Please let me go. I promise I won't tell on you. I'll say I ran away, then got scared and came home again."

But Jace ignores her.

"Right, now we're all ready to go."

He flings her back on the mattress and she allows him to do with her, as he will. She screams as the barrel of the rifle penetrates her, its raised sight tearing tender tissue. He pushes it deep within the young girl who hears no more, as she passes out before the weapon is fired up towards her brain.

"Well, enjoyed that, didn't we?"

Jace grins in satisfaction as he ejaculates over the damaged body of an innocent child. A perverted man, made so perhaps by his unfortunate childhood, but nevertheless, undeniably an evil murderer.

Then he rolls her body onto a plastic sheet.

He moves the table and pulls the rug to one side, revealing a trapdoor. Opening it, he drops the rifle down and mentally counts to five before hearing it splash into the sewer below, the body parts will follow later. He closes the trap again, pulling the rug back over it.

"The cellar must be neat and tidy.
The cellar must be perfectly clean."

Jace can still hear his father repeating that mantra the night his mother died. He shivers at the memory.

"Yes, father."

He collects cleaning materials from the storage cupboard, and omitting to close the panel, proceeds to scrub walls and floor. Then, moving the body in its plastic sheet to the floor, he tries to clean the mattress with a stain remover.

What's that?

Low down on the wall, Emma has scratched her name and then in quotes "JANITOR".

"Fuckin' bitch! How dare she!"

He is shouting and aiming a savage kick at the bed misses and stumbles backwards. Grabbing the tabletop, Jace bangs his head onto it again and again, finally falling onto the still-damp mattress, wiping blood where it drips from his eyebrow. Now prostrate on his back, his ice-blue eyes are trance-blank.

~~

Ten minutes later, when Ami returns to the janitor's workshop during the lunch break, there is no sign of Jace.

Where the hell is he?

"Jace…Jace!" she calls, but receiving no reply, enters the boiler room. It is dark and a bit creepy, but Ami knows her way around, and eerie though it might be, Jace does keep it clean and neat.

"A place for everything and everything in its place." She grimaces, recalling Jace's obsession with tidiness.

There is a dim light showing from the storage cupboard, so Ami makes her way towards it. She moves quietly, if Jace is trying to avoid her, she will surprise him and make him jump.

'That's funny, I've not seen that before.'

Ami reaches the open panel and sees steps leading down. She goes down the first two steps, then bends forward to see more clearly into the room…

"Aagh! Jace!" she screams at the sight before her.

Her screams reverberate throughout the boiler room. Jace's eyes flash back to life as he springs towards her. Ami turns, pulling her foot free of the hand that grabs her, but Jace is fit, quicker and as she reaches the open door of the storage cupboard, he leaps forward and brings her down.

His weight drives the air from her body and Ami has difficulty regaining her breath.

Jace turns her over, his heavy body squashing her breasts. He catches her flailing hands, holding them easily above her head. But Ami is not done yet, her legs are free but she keeps them still, waiting for the right moment. Then drives her right knee with all the force she can muster, into his most tender region.

"Got you, you bastard."

The resulting pain causes Jace to release his hold and bend double, clutching the affected area. He is incapacitated sufficiently for Ami to wriggle free, but Jace summons enough strength to grab her ankle. Ami kicks his face hard with the other foot. Grabbing his hair in both hands, she raises his head, yelling, "Take that, you psycho-crazy!" And thumps it down on the concrete floor.

～～

Three boys lolling behind the boiler house to sneak a smoke during their lunchtime break have heard Ami's screams. Hastily crushing out their cigarettes, they all run to find a teacher, to report the screams. Mr Jenkins was the duty primary and they found him sitting on a wall in the playground.

"Sir! Sir! Somebody's screaming in the boiler house, sir…we just heard them! It sounds like someone's being murdered, sir."

Mr Jenkins' immediate inclination is to ask the boys what they are doing near the boiler house, which is out of bounds. But the answer is obvious and more important things need to be done. He immediately contacts the police inspector who with his team is already on site, still conducting their investigation into the disappearance of Emma.

~~

Breaking free at last, Ami runs out into the blessed daylight, into the arms of a policewoman and safety.

"He tried to kill me. He's mad. His eyes were all staring. I think there's another body in there." Ami's voice is verging on hysteria and the policewoman is gentle, calming her until an ambulance arrives.

"Who do you mean, miss?"

~~

Jace, handcuffed and accompanied by two policemen, stops and glares at her.

"You were special," he snarls. "Not a brat to control and rape. You were s'posed to be like my Ma, She cleaned up after the Old Man, no bloodstains, everythin' neat'n clean. I was trainin' you…was goin' to marry you. We would've had a son and I would've been Top Dog like the Old Man meant me to be. He showed me all the ways to catch 'em. How to chain 'em, do 'em, kill 'em."

> *"The cellar must be neat and tidy.*
> *The cellar must be perfectly clean."*

"Didn't know what happened. Emm, didn't…friggin' sex blew her bloody head off."

His laugh is that of a madman, terrifying.

"Come on, in you get."

The policeman grimaces with disdain as he pushes Jace into the van.

The court case and judicial commitment will follow, with all the media publicity involved.

So no change there!

Gramps' Glass

Time itself is different in the parallel universe.

"Gramps, can I clear the brambles and stuff from behind the shed? There's something at the back that's shiny and sort of wobbly."

"No!" I said it fiercely, and I felt dreadful as Tom's face fell. I could see the bewildered, frightened face of a ten-year-old behind that of the handsome youth of sixteen, standing before me. His parents had both been killed in an air crash when he was ten. He had been at boarding school at the time and chose to stay there, but Wayend Cottage is his home, and he will inherit it in due time, just as I had done.

"I'm sorry, Tom. Didn't mean to bark at you."

I thought about it for a while, as we looked each other directly in the eye. Tom was now the same age as I had been when…

"The time has come for us to have a good old chat about what is behind that shed, boy. Let's get a mug of tea first though, for it will be thirsty work."

Twenty minutes later…

"Is it to do with that flickering stuff that's all covered with weeds? I bet it is!"

"Yes, boy, you're right about that but there's much more to tell. You see, it's all to do with this family, the Morgans. But let's start at the beginning. I was eighteen when I inherited Wayend. When I found the amulet and made my second trip through the glass gateway to the parallel universe beyond."

"A parallel universe, Gramps? You mean there actually are such things? I've read about the possibility in science magazines but surely, they're like black holes, merely conjecture."

"They exist, Tom, but let me tell it in my own way…questions afterwards, okay?"

Tom nodded his assent and made a closing zip action across his lips.

~~~

It was 1956 and I just couldn't believe Gramps was dead. That'd be your great-great-grandfather. We stood at the graveside, Mum and Dad on either side of me as the vicar rambled on. *What's the matter with you, God?* I thought. *You know it's too soon for Gramps.*

But I knew that wasn't right, Gramps would be happy again, he'd gone back through the glass, and now whatever followed would be down to me.

I clenched my teeth and chewed at my lip, anything to stop me from crying like Mum was, she'd loved her father deeply and he would be a great loss. Dad had his arm round her, so I took hold of her hand and squeezed it gently.

We went back to Wayend after the funeral, with all the relatives and most of the village, and it wasn't until they were all settled with their cups of tea or glasses of Gramps' best whiskey, that I was able to escape into the garden.

I sat under the weeping willow, in my special place, yours now, boy, and at last, was able to howl my grief out. Then I went over what had happened. The stories he told were hard to believe but I knew he would never lie to me.

~~

Gramps had been the best grandfather in the world. Gramma had died when I was just a baby, so I don't really remember her but Gramps used to look after me once I started school. My mum and dad were both solicitors, with their own firm, and most of my holidays were spent with Gramps here at Wayend Cottage.

Now Gramps was gone too and all he told me, had become my responsibility.

Like he had all those years ago, I sat under the weeping willow and like him, I howled out my grief. When I had no more tears, I went through what I had discovered about the parallel universe that lay behind Gramps' Glass.

~~

It all started when I was five, summer holidays and the first time I'd stayed at Wayend Cottage without my mum. I'm rather ashamed to say that I didn't miss her one bit.

Gramps and I went fishing in the lake. That was when we named it Rainbow Lake, for as you know, when it rains and there's a bit of sun in the sky, there's nearly always a beautiful rainbow stretched across it. We rambled through the nearby woods where Gramps told me the names of trees, what fungi were safe to eat and which ones were poisonous. I learnt about all sorts of interesting things. He knew so much about so many things, from nature to science, and at night, we would look through his old brass telescope and he would tell me the names of the stars.

One day though, when I was nearly six, Gramps said he had some work to do, so I took a book into the garden, under the willow tree.

Anyway, I read for a while, then got bored and went to pick an apple. There used to be a tree by the old garden shed that was weighed down with Beauty of Bath apples. They were tangy sweet and juicy, with flashes of pink in their flesh and were the ones I liked best. As I reached up to pick the fruit, I was dazzled by something glinting behind the shed, so shoving a couple in my pocket and biting into a third, I squeezed into the gap and could see what looked like glass but it was sort of wobbling and blurry. There were loads of stinging nettles behind the shed and after I had stung my legs and arms, I gave up and went to find some dock leaves to take the sting out.

I remembered the glass when we were having tea and asked Gramps about it.

He said, "Oh, that'll be some old windows I've got stored there with the sun reflecting off them. Now, don't you go fishing around, some of it's probably broken by now and you could get a real bad cut."

I told him sure, I didn't want to get stung any more, it hurt.

No more was said on that subject but the next time I stayed with him, there was a stout wooden fence across the gap between the shed and the back wall.

~~

But as I said, I inherited Wayend when I was eighteen and going through Gramps things then, reminded me of my first trip through the glass gateway in the summer holidays two years earlier.

Gramps was getting old, and his arthritis had been playing up. Sometimes he was alright, but quite often, his hands were so painful he would get out a bottle of whiskey and sit in his chair with a science magazine on his knee. But he didn't read it, for within a few minutes his eyes closed, and he'd fall asleep.

That day, I went out into the garden but instead of going to my den, I stood on a box and looked over the fence that closed off the back of the shed. It was still there, Gramps' Glass, still shimmering and wobbling, just like it had ten years before.

But I wasn't six years old now. I was sixteen, almost grown up. So I went into the shed and found some shears, then scrambled over the fence and cut the nettles down, making a clear path to the glass.

For a while, I stood and watched the strange effect, then tapped the side of the glass with the shears. It didn't sound quite like when you tap on a window, I couldn't really describe it. I rapped my fingers on the centre of the glass and it felt as though they pushed into it, almost as though it was not solid glass but a plastic bag full of water. Placing my hand, palm down on the glass, I pushed. I gasped as my hand disappeared, I pulled and breathed a sigh of relief as it appeared again, still firmly attached to my right arm, and apparently not damaged. I tried again, with the same result, so feeling braver, I disappeared my foot. This needed thinking through though, so I withdrew it and went back to the old willow den, where I closed my eyes and munched an apple. It only took me twenty minutes to make up my mind…but in all honesty, I guess I'd already done that when I was still behind the shed.

Returning to the house, I found Gramps sound asleep and snoring gently, so bearing in mind that he and I were always truthful with each other and not wanting him to worry about my absence, I wrote him a note telling him what I was about to do.

Yes, of course, it was thoughtless.

Not worry…of course, he would but when you're young, you don't always think things through properly.

This time, as I stood close to the glass, it seemed to shiver faster. Then it changed. As I put my right foot forward, the shivering became a whirlpool. I leaned forward, feeling with the foot I could no longer see, for solid ground and was sucked into the whirlpool. I spun clockwise twice, then felt myself falling, rolling down a steep slope, where I eventually came to a painful stop against a gorse bush.

I was nearly at the bottom of a steep slope overlooking a lake. Water of bright-coloured rainbow stripes rippled from side to side and in the centre was a rock, standing about a metre above water level. The rock was an ominous black against the brightness of the lake and sat upon it was a mermaid.

No honestly! You must believe me. She was perched there brushing long blond tresses forward, covering her naked top half. The lower half was, of course, a fishtail, which picked up the rainbow from the water and glinted through the spectrum of colours like the spinning mirror sphere at a disco.

I stood there for I don't know how long.

"What d'you think you're staring at?"

The angry voice behind me made me jump, and I turned to see a scowling boy of about my own age. He was wearing shorts, a black tee shirt with a motif that reminded me of the whirling motion as I came through Gramps' Glass and sandals without socks.

"I'm Jamie Todsworth, who're you?"

"Tom Morgan."

"Hey! That's Gramps' name too, not Tom, he's *Nicholas* Morgan." Jamie had thick dark hair that needed cutting and seemed to have an aggressive life of its own. His eyes looked almost black as they flashed, surveying first me and then the lake, as though expecting someone else to appear.

Feeling I had to say something, I said the first thing that came into my head.

"Hi Jamie, what is this place?"

"New Ways, of course, stupid, and that's Rainbow Lake. Everybody around here knows that."

I paused, trying to make up my mind whether or not to tell him about my trip through the glass doorway. We looked at each other and I liked what I saw. Jamie's eyes were dark brown, clear, and intelligent and I felt an instant comradeship with him. He obviously felt the same, for he grinned at me, revealing even white teeth and his face seemed to light up from within. I'd made up my mind.

"You might not believe me, Jamie, but I swear what I'm going to tell you is true."

So I revealed how I had come through Gramps' Glass. When I paused for breath, he could stay quiet no longer.

"Wow! That's magic! I live with my gramma at New Ways Cottage. Come on up with me and meet her. Gramma has mentioned something about a parallel world, but she will never tell me more. We've got some lemonade and I don't know about you but I'm thirsty. Gramma makes the best lemonade you ever tasted."

I thought that was a good idea, so we climbed back up the slope to Jamie's home, which from the outside seemed very similar to Wayend Cottage, except for a fenced platform on the roof overlooking the lake. However, there was no wall behind the shed at the bottom of New Ways Cottage garden, just a rather scrappy hedge about thirty centimetres high and I realised that was how I had come to fall down the slope. The glass gateway had to be the shed window, which was shimmering but wasn't wobbly like Gramps' Glass and appeared to reach from just below the roof to ground level. I discovered later that to get back to my world, it was necessary to use the glass gateway from the inside of the shed, where it was easier to see it was wobbly. Anyone looking at the window from outside would think it was just natural reflection.

Gramma proved to be an old lady, though younger than Gramps and looked very much like a photo that was kept on our piano. Jamie introduced us, and she looked at me so intensely that I thought she was reading my thoughts. She must have been too.

"You should not have come through the glass, Tom," she said. "It is not time yet. How is your Gramps, dear?"

It sounded as if she knew him, but how could she? Then it clicked they must have met through the glass, like Jamie and me.

"He's mostly fine but his arthritis gets painful, and he tries to squelch it with whiskey then he goes to sleep, have you met him?" I gabbled without taking a breath.

The old lady chuckled.

"Yes dear, many years ago, he took me through the glass into his world, but I was only able to stay there for thirty years, and then I had to come back here. That's the rule."

"Where is 'here'?"

"This is New Ways Cottage on the outskirts of New Ways village on First Parallel, which is the largest of the parallel universes, and nearest to your world. Let me pour you some lemonade and I'll try to explain."

Jamie was right it was the best I ever tasted.

"Your gramps first came through the glass when he was in his early thirties. He'd inherited Wayend Cottage the year before and when he got down to tidying the garden, he found the 'glass gateway' behind the shed. I suppose you did the same, and found out that you can get through. We met that first time and fell in love but I couldn't go back with him then."

She paused, thinking back, then continued, "It was five years before he could get through again, the glass is not always ready to let someone come here, you see but that time, I *was* able to return with him."

She looked sad.

"Weren't you happy about that?"

"Yes, dear. Only someone from the direct Morgan line, who comes from your world, can visit First Parallel through the gateway and if they follow the rules, they can return again. However, some people from the parallel universe are occasionally allowed to go withershins." She paused, recalling, looking backwards to her memories, but only if someone very close to the visitor from your world can replace them.

Your gramps knew the rules of First Parallel, so didn't expect to ever get me out in his lifetime, and he wanted a family. So he married a lovely girl named Merrill in your world. Then she died giving birth to our Jamie, and about a year later, Nicholas came through and took me back with him. We were so happy. I was thirty-three and your gramps thirty-seven when your mother was born. Then she grew up, married your father and a year later you were born. Unfortunately, the thirty-year rule came into effect very soon after your birth and I had to return.

Now you had best be getting back or the glass on this side will close and you'll be stuck. Jamie dear, show Tom the way, please.

That was curious. Jamie had, at no point, inferred that he knew about the glass gateway and I could not contain my curiosity.

"Why didn't you say you knew about the glass, Jamie?"

"Because I'm not supposed to talk about it to anyone…ever. Gramma and I and now you know about it but we must never ever speak of it, not even to each other. There is a reason for that but I don't know what it is 'cos she won't tell me. But perhaps Gramma will tell both of us when you get to come back here again. You will try and come again, won't you?"

"You bet I will. This is the best adventure of my life."

We were nearly at the shed when I asked Jamie where his mother was. He looked sad and pointed to the rock in the lake, shaking his head. I understood that he didn't want to talk about it and anyway, we had reached the garden shed. To my surprise, when Jamie opened the door, which was firmly locked, the interior was not full of garden equipment, like Gramps', but was a well-fitted office, containing a desk on which sat a computer with all its paraphernalia and shelves of books and files. The long window I had seen from the outside was covered by a purple roller blind, which Jamie hastened to raise.

"Quick, the ripples are changing."

The appearance of the glass had indeed changed the wobbly pattern was getting cloudy and the undulations were much slower. It had that still dark brown colour you get just before it snows. I pushed the two apples from my pocket into Jamie's hands and he gave me a shove into the glass. I spun twice, in an anti-clockwise direction this time and landed on my back behind Gramps' shed. He was standing there, looking scared out of his wits. I felt a tightening around my foot and found I could not move it. The glass was almost still now, just a sheet of dirty, cloudy glass. Gramps caught me under the arms and pulled, but my foot was firmly stuck.

"Pull your foot out of that damned sneaker," he roared.

That was all it took to reawaken my brain and I wriggled my foot free of the shoe. As I did so, the glass closed over the footwear and breathing a sigh of relief Gramps and I hugged, then with our arms around each other, we went into the house.

After dinner that night, Gramps told me about his trip to New Ways and how he had fallen in love with Gramma.

"There is something else I have to tell you about the parallel universes, Tom, and I'm not quite sure how to put it."

"Mum and Dad? Is that it, Gramps? Is that where people go when they're...dead?"

"Kind of...but not everyone gets to stay on the first parallel universe, like I said at the beginning, it's something special to the direct Morgan line. Your mum would have been allowed to stay if she wanted, but I expect she would have chosen to go on with your father to the second one. I shall definitely stay there when it's my time and you will be able to if you want, for you are my only next of kin. It's a good job you are a boy though, a girl has to have completed a quest to be allowed to stay. That is what happened to Merrill, she obviously wanted to stay with her son, Jamie, but someone did not want that to happen. I wonder why?"

~~

Then Gramps died, I inherited Wayend Cottage and that is when I knew I would go back through Gramps' Glass.

That night, I dreamed about the parallel universe. I was trying to get back into my own world, time was running out and something was holding me back from the glass, trying to stop me from returning. I felt myself thump loose and awoke to find I had rolled out of bed. It was daylight and the birds were singing, so although it was only five o'clock, I dressed and went down to fix some breakfast.

Then I decided to go through some of the things in Gramps' study.

I found the box at the back of a cupboard, mostly it contained old magazines and astronomy papers, but I went carefully through the lot in case something important turned up. I wasn't expecting anything, really, but right at the bottom was a small, padded envelope, carefully sealed with sticky tape. I ran a sharp blade along the top, opening it carefully. To my surprise, it contained a gold amulet hung on a leather bootlace, depicting a mermaid sitting on a rock. The amulet was warm to the touch and as I lifted it from the tissue wrapping, the feeling that went through my hand was like that shivering shock when a fish bites. A ripple, a tingle, and a burst of pure excitement. It was about the size of an old half-crown coin and the back was engraved with words that I recognised as Latin.

"Non omnis moriar
Resurgam hostis humani generis
Malo animo."

I translated it and was pleased it proved to be correct when I checked later.

"I shall not wholly die
I shall rise again
With evil intent."

What on earth did it mean? What reference can the ominous words on the back have to the mermaid? Gramps had told me about the amulet he'd found on the shores of Rainbow Lake. That had been when he was just a young man in his mid-twenties when he first discovered the gateway through the glass. He always said the amulet had been lost, so why was it sealed in an envelope and concealed at the bottom of the box? Had he forgotten about it? I would not think so, knowing Gramps as I had. We were always very close, and Wayend Cottage was now my responsibility. Gramps would expect me to follow through because he knew I had, still have, an inquisitive turn of mind…he frequently reminded me that curiosity killed the cat.

Yes! Gramps would be waiting for my visit.

Eventually, I stopped asking myself questions, slipped the leather thong over my head and tucked the amulet inside my T-shirt. I would find out the next time I went through Gramps' Glass into the parallel universe but at that time, I had no idea of its significance.

~~

I did, of course, go back through the glass and as you see, I returned safely but that was allowed because of the quest. I was there for some time but as I said before, time is different in the parallel universe, it seems to run to suit any occasion. So far as this world was concerned, I was only away for a day but it had to be many weeks in that strange place. But I know the parallel rules and I can't return again, until the final visit, when I shall have to stay.

When I have a grandson and am a gramps myself, I shall tell him everything and risk breaking the first parallel rules…or shall I?

When I asked, "Did you have adventures there, Gramps?"

His reply was, "I did but can't tell, it's parallel rules."

"Shall I be able to go through and look for Mum and Dad?"

"Tom, it is not that easy. You can't take the risk. I'm sorry but you *must* wait until Wayend is yours and you can do as you wish."

~~

I loved my Gramps dearly, so have to inevitably wait as he says I must but the time will come when I can travel through what I call Gramps' Glass into the parallel universe. Above all, I will certainly see Gramps again, and meet Great-Great Gramps and Gramma, and Jamie. Will he still be a boy like me? I think he will because of the strange things that happen in the parallel universe. Perhaps I will find Mum and Dad…that would be great.

It is a comfort to know that when the end comes, I shall be able to go through Gramps' Glass gateway and be with those I love, who have preceded me to the parallel universe. But for the time being, I must wait…

Pig in a Poke

"We got another bloody pig stuck in the pipe last night."

Tom raised his eyebrows, glancing around at his five companions.

Jerry's glass of cider was halfway to his mouth, frozen in time like Lot's wife. Karen's hands were over her mouth as though to stifle a scream, Adam looked no different from normal, his mouth agape, eyes protuberant, he always seemed to breathe through his mouth, anyway. Ben's hands were pressed palms down on the table, as though levering himself into a standing position, ready to attack. Laura, lips pressed tightly together, nostrils flared, glared through her narrow spectacles at the man sitting at the next table, if looks could kill. They were first-year students and sole members of the newly formed Animal Rights Society, known to some as the ARSes.

"Now do you believe me?" Tom asked the group of anti-vivisection wannabes.

Ben pushed himself up. "We have to talk to him. Find out more, so we can plan our attack and rescue."

"I'm sure we all agree with that," Karen's quiet voice broke in, "but we must be careful. I think Tom should make the approach, after all, he was the one to discover this horrible act of cruelty."

The others agreed, Ben somewhat reluctantly, but he knew he was overruled and clicking his fingers towards the bar yelled, "Same again here!" He stood up and then sat down again. The fresh drinks arrived, and he pointed to Adam. "Your call this time."

Adam shrugged and paid up. Ben was good at this. Adam couldn't remember when Ben last actually paid for a round of drinks, he was a master of monetary avoidance.

They discussed strategy and when one of the men at the next table left, Tom moved into his place.

"Excuse me," he said, "I'm Tom Lucas. I apologise for my cheek, but I couldn't help overhearing you saying you had a pig stuck in a pipe. You work for the oil company, don't you? How on earth did a pig manage to get into the pipe in the first place? Surely, the company has to seal all pipes against such eventualities."

John Whittaker smiled at the young man before him. "Not at all, Tom. My name is John. Do sit down and I'll try to explain."

Tom sat, flicking a triumphant glance towards his friends. An action not missed by the devious engineer.

John drained his glass. "You want to talk about the oil industry?"

Tom nodded.

"Well, when the oil arrives from Saudi Arabia and other places, it's what they call crude oil, which means to say that it's not pure oil. It's got a certain amount of sludge in it, the same sort of thing you get in your car engine when you change your oil. It's not all gooey, you know, but it's got bits in it, and some of these solids when you pump them through a pipeline, say a hundred miles long, are going to fall out of the oil and coat around the inside of the pipe. Plus the fact that there's a certain amount of bacteria in the oil and these bacteria stay with the sludge."

"Yes, I get it, but what about the pigs?"

"I'm just coming to that, but I need a drink."

Tom hurriedly went to the bar, returning with a pint of lager and half-pint of cider.

"Thanks, Son."

John drank half his beer, settled himself comfortably and continued.

"As I said, you get a coating of sludge on the pipe, so periodically you have to clean them out. We do them on a pretty regular basis, can't let the pipes get blocked. You have to shut off the oil and put a pig through the pipes, using compressed air. Erm! And there are various places in the pipe where you can get the pig out. They're a bit like branch lines. These side pipes are called pokes. So if you put the door at an angle to the pipe, the pig coming out of the pipe gets shoved into one of these pokes. Hence the expression a pig in a poke. Pigs are the bane of an engineer's life."

John sighed, quaffed another long draft of beer and buried his bulbous nose in a large off-white handkerchief that looked as if he might have used it to clean some errant sludge from his hands. Having examined its contents, he stuffed the offending rag back in the pocket of his tweed jacket, saying, "Come on, lad, drink up it's my call."

John made a surprisingly light-footed pathway for such a cumbersome man, to the bar. He returned at very short shrift plonking the full glasses down. Leaving splashes of liquid spangles and rings like miniature moats where they stood.

"Why? Why are pigs the bane of your life?"

I remember one draughtsman was told to design a poke at the top of an incline and, like I said, the pig is deflected into the poke. When the door opens, the pig comes out. Unfortunately, the silly bugger did it pointing upwards. Well, the pipers and welders didn't give a toss where it was, so they just followed the plan. So when we did the test run, once the pig was in the poke, we gave it an extra burst of compressed air, and when the bloody thing came out of the poke, it was shot up into the air like a bullet from a gun. Didn't last for long, of course. Gravity had its way. Brought the pig back to earth again after about half a mile. Talk about flying pigs! Haha!

That's one thing we do if it gets stuck, give it a nudge with an extra-strong blast of compressed air. But if you still can't move the blasted thing, then there's always the wire rope that we hook onto the tail end. That's something I don't want to even think about though. You can spend frigging hours pulling and tugging it back and then if the tail breaks off, you're in dead trouble."

He sighed and emptied his glass with his head held back to imbibe the very last drop.

"That's about the most embarrassing thing for an engineer though, to get a pig stuck in a pipe."

Tom glanced at his friends at the other table. They were obviously totally engrossed, and he noticed that Karen was taking notes and Adam appeared to still be intent on catching any insects willing to fly into his open mouth. He thought it was time to ask another question.

"When do you usually put the pigs in the pipes? I mean, is there a special time you like…feed them the sludge?"

"Usually at the end of an oil run, when it's been pumped through a pipeline to a destination, then we automatically do a pig run. For instance, there'll be one about midnight tonight on the line between Fawley and Bristol. Now that's a long one and we have some ten pokes on that line."

"So the pigs have to go all the way from Fawley to Bristol. How many are there in that pipeline?"

"Depends. If it's been a fairly clean run, probably one for each poke, but if it's been a really dirty crude, then we'll decide at the start of the run. Anyway." He drained his glass. "That's what happened today, must be off to the pipeline, see if we can blast it back the way it came. One bloody thing after another."

He wound his way through the crowded pub to the car park. The students quickly followed, trying to keep a low profile. They parked out of sight and made their way to the start of the pipeline, where it was hoped they would be able to photograph the exit of the pig.

~~

Half an hour later, six very dirty students returned to Tom's car. The engineer in charge had lectured them on trespass, then unable to keep a straight face any longer spluttered, "Pigs! Bloody pigs!"

John reckoned he wouldn't need to buy a pint for many weeks to come. He could drink to his heart's content on that yarn.

The Power of Mr Aquba

Sium Aquba was a small man. Well, he would be. He was, after all, a pygmy. Not only that. He was the son of Chief Ecansium who happened to also be the shaman of the tribe.

They lived in the Serenwatever and were known as the Wethefucarwee Tribe.

Grasses grew tall in the Serenwatever, taller than the pygmies, who were frequently to be seen springing vertically in the air whilst shouting the tribal name. This practice was, of course, necessary, to enable them to ensure they were going in the prescribed direction.

Chief Ecansium Aquba had been chosen for two reasons. The first was that he was said to be the oldest member of the tribe, having told everyone he was at this time, 103 years old. Secondly, he could jump higher than anyone else. He was also a very clever man and could always be certain of talking others into his way of thinking. That is power. Power is money and money is yet more power, bringing with it advantages. After all, this was the twenty-first century.

The chief smiled but only to himself. Other members of his tribe had never seen this amazing transformation of their leader's facial muscles and he made sure they never would. Ecansium could hardly believe how easy it was to keep the tribe within the confines of the Dark Ages. A little hokum-pokum kept them in nervous thrall of him. He was a very adept illusionist and, had he wished, could have performed on stage worldwide. His stiff facial muscles performed once more, producing rather a sneer than a smile. For although the tribe gave him the necessary power, it was his laptop computer that served to make him rich.

For two months each year, March and August, Chief Ecansium went on what he told the tribe was a 'walkabout'. During these months, so he told them, he met with the 'Great Spirit' for a renewal of strength and to report on the behaviour of tribal members. This not only enabled him to escape the sometimes rather boring village confines but ensured that everyone behaved themselves, fearing that a bad report to the Great Spirit might bring the wrath of that personage down upon them.

When he left, the whole tribe was always gathered in the communal meeting-house. There they stayed in fear and trembling until the whirring roar of the Great Spirit had diminished into the distance, taking with him Chief Ecansium Aquba. Then normal life would continue for precisely twenty-eight days and nights, when once again, they would all ensconce themselves in the meeting-house and await the roar of the Great Spirit. This time nobody would leave, no matter how long a time until their chief joined them. He would shower them with gifts and draw lollipops from the ears of children. Then he would pour milk from his glass jug, the only one in the village, into a white man's paper on which was illegible printing (but which the tribe knew their shaman could through his magic, read). Having ascertained from his audience that everyone had seen the milk pour from the jug into the paper, he screwed the latter into a ball and threw it at a young man standing at the back of the group. There were gasps of amazement, as it became apparent that the crumpled paper was not only empty of milk but also dry. Where had it gone? The young man, surrounded now by other young tribesmen, the women being obliged to keep quiet on the outskirts, slowly straightened the paper. Finally, satisfied that there was no sign of milk therein, he led the applause and cheers for their wonderful shaman and his undoubted magic. Finally, power renewed, and gullibility ensured, the people were dispersed and Ecansium returned to his hut.

Now Ecansium's hut looked exactly like all the others on the outside, except that it had a door, rather than the usual drape of plaited grass. This door also contained a strong lock, the key to which hung from a cord around Ecansium's neck which, of course, was also gazed upon by the tribe as shaman magic. However, the inside was as different as chalk and cheese. For a start, the floor was covered with a splendid Persian carpet. It was also furnished with a comfortable couch and leather-covered desk. On the desk rested a battery-operated laptop computer and inkjet printer. Within the drawers were a fresh stock of batteries, ink refills, private business papers and stationery.

Only one person other than Ecansium was allowed in this hut. That was his number one wife, Shutim. On one day per week, Shutim would be allowed to enter and thoroughly clean the hut, for which she received the honour of being serviced by her master. For her perpetual silence regarding the contents of this private place, she secured his promise that she would, for all time, continue to hold her position over the other five wives. This put Shutim in a very powerful position of her own and Ecansium had no worries on this score, for she was nearly thirty years of age, being much older than the other wives who were all aged between twelve and sixteen, young and beautiful.

However, it was Shutim who bore his firstborn. Sium was not only smaller than average but seemed to have little ability in the skill of jumping. His father encouraged him, then beat him but nothing could induce a skill that was non-existent. However, like his father, he was a clever boy and by the time he was five, had persuaded his mother to smuggle him into Ecansium's private hut. But his father discovered him there, playing Minesweeper on the computer, which ensured that Sium was sent away to be educated in Johannesburg, where he attended a very upmarket boarding school run by Jesuit monks. Whilst there, he comported himself with diligent integrity, which eventually earned him a place in one of England's top universities.

Within two years, Sium had won an honours degree in Social Economics and Mathematics. Concurrently, he also obtained a degree in Twentieth Century World History but only a B1 in this subject.

Sium loved university life, where he had made many friends, with whom he spent enjoyable holidays at their family estates and learnt to speak with an English upper-class accent. So much did he enjoy himself that he was able to persuade his father to support him for another two years or so. This time, his chosen subject was Particle Physics, in which he later obtained a PhD.

So now, at the tender age of twenty-five, Sium considered what to do with his future.

His desire was to be rich, richer than his father, and independent of him. This naturally led him to join the London Stock Exchange.

As was his normal manner, Sium paid attention to everything going on around him and applied himself to any task given him with great diligence. Within six months, he was introduced to the art of dealing and by the end of his first year at the Stock Exchange, he was a top futures dealer.

Now all this time spent studying and subsequently working, did not diminish Sium's social life. He still kept in touch with his university friends and seemed only to need a couple of hours sleep each night. Thus he wined, dined and clubbed with the best of 'em, refusing to experiment with heroin, ecstasy, or any other heavier or lighter drugs offered him. On the other hand, he privately indulged in his own secret supply, sent to him on a regular basis by his father.

This was naturally, generally unknown and customs had never found any substance to cause suspicion. Therein, of course, lay his overwhelming successes.

Then, Sium received an e-mail from his father's internet connection. It was not from Chief Ecansium but from his number one wife, Shutim and it informed him that his father had gone to join his ancestors in the great beyond for the last time. In other words, he was dead. You should return immediately, his mother had written. Shutim was not stupid and had a pretty good idea of what her husband had been up to. During his absences, she made use of his computer and taught herself to read so that she could understand the other aspects of his life, returning to the subservient wife on his return.

But Sium had no desire or intention of returning to tribal life and advised his mother of his decision.

~~

This is how, at the usual time of the year, in August, the tribe retreated to the meeting-house, where they stayed until the roar of the Great Spirit faded away. They stayed there for two days thereafter, trying to choose from amongst them, the next chief.

But Shutim was not with them this time. As the number one wife of the late Chief Ecansium Aquba, she was allowed to mourn alone in his private hut, after which she was supposed to prepare it for the possession of the next chief.

The computers and boxes of valuables accrued by her husband were packed into trunks and loaded by Sium and his mother into the helicopter.

One has to assume that they both lived happily together in Sium's English Mansion house but perhaps relieved of the chains of marriage, Shutim chose to control the lives of both herself and her son.

The tribe? Who knows!

The Old Inn Cottage

Part I

Mortise locks! I don't mean the kind we get nowadays for the back door, small aluminium things. No indeedy! I am referring to the type used for doors made of a solid slab of oak. Church doors, Tudor doors, solid and heavy, you know what I mean? The key to such a lock was huge, fifteen centimetres long, with a hollow elliptical top and a castellated operating bit of about one and a half centimetres square. Heavy too, much heavier to carry around than a modern mobile phone. It was perhaps heavier than my purse, with its inevitable collection of twenty-first century small coinage. Turning that key in the lock was for me, a two handed job.

The cottage was of Tudor vintage, with inset beams in mud and daub walls that were a full meter thick. The front door with its small porch, led directly onto the village road and entered directly into a large living room with a small, fixed lattice window. Set halfway down the right-hand side was a granite fireplace large enough to take over-sized logs. In the far right-hand corner was a door, complete with Suffolk latch, which proved to open onto a twisting stairway.

In the left-hand wall was an opening that led to another room, slightly smaller than the first and with no windows whatsoever. Electricity had been installed, after a fashion, and a bare bulb revealed an old range in an inglenook. It was never used other than for boiling a cast-iron kettle that my husband and I named Great Bess. I could tip it to fill a mug but no way could I lift it when full of water. I loved that range though, except when it became necessary to black-lead the wretched thing. There was a cellar, which was entered from a small cupboard in that room but had been mostly filled in. When and by whom, we were unable to discover.

Another doorless opening led into a scullery containing a large earthenware sink, over which hung, somewhat precariously, a tap attached to a lead pipe.

Totally illegal nowadays, of course, but we did replace the lead with copper pipework. In a recess by the back door was a small Aga cooker, much in need of a thorough cleaning. The kitchen was more like a lean-to as the roof in the front was built from the second floor, whilst at the back it extended from the peak to the back door level.

Climbing the stairs was something to be done with care. Because they were curved. Each step was full width on the right and narrowed to about 4" on the left and each was nearly 15" tall. However, they felt firm enough.

Upstairs were two bedrooms with 1" thick by 10" wide floorboards and lattice windows with window seats let into the thick walls. Both rooms boasted plank doors with Suffolk latches.

Then, I discovered another such door, which was perhaps three-quarters the height of the others on that small square landing. I opened it tentatively. Just as well too, for there was a step down into a room, which appeared to be full of various pieces of wood, paper and horror of horrors: HUGE SPIDERS. They were pink, the room allowing no daylight to enter through the slanting roof. I have never seen a larger arachnid. That step, by the way, was half a metre down, so mind your head and don't fall! But that was not discovered until after a full week of bundling up rubbish and carting it down the narrow, steep stairs to the bonfire. It turned out to be a bathroom, containing a small washbasin and old zinc bathtub, plus a hot water tank, which proved to be connected to the Aga below. I hesitate to even guess for what or when the previous inhabitant had used it.

The loft proved to be most interesting though. In it was discovered a hidey-hole, but more of that later.

In the end, the Old Inn Cottage received an extra window in the room with the range, which became a cosy dining room, plus a renovated kitchen. What was apparently the bathroom, received a slanting window, which was let into the roof but was otherwise just thoroughly cleaned for the time being. After much hard scrubbing and painting, some carpets and furniture, it eventually became home. Nevertheless, all the time we lived there, that cottage held a feeling of menace for me. There was always that strange tapping in the loft. I would say, bravely I thought, 'Oh shut up, Gilbert!' The surprising thing was that he did. *Gilbert the Ghost.* We never saw anything, only heard and noted that the tapping stopped when I spoke. A tuned-in death-watch-beetle, perhaps!

By the way, the toilet was outside, built onto the side of the kitchen against the outside wall, an old-fashioned Elson, which we emptied by digging holes at the bottom of the garden, making sure not to use the same place twice. We tried not to empty our bowels until we were at work.

The garden? I leave that to your imagination…long and ragged. It was eventually sorted, but never seriously claimed from nature.

~~

Part II

"Careful now, watch your step."

Planks had been laid across the adze-cut beams and bright halogen lights erected throughout the loft, dispensing a brightness that seemed to me only to accentuate the cobwebs that now fluttered, broken by the SOCO team.

~~

"Go on then, move."

"Hang on. Ugh! It's full of webs and who knows what nasty things up here. Okay, you can come up now."

He joined me in the loft, pulling himself up by the strength of his arms, took the torch and made his way first to the water tank. There was no cover and he fished out a couple of dead pigeons, whilst I swallowed a scream at the sight of a dead rat between the beams. In the torch beam, a large space was revealed, apparently empty of all but things that choose to live in the dark. We will need to remove the rodent bodies, from which the malodorous waves were emitted, but that is for another day, when we will equip ourselves with a suitable bag (double bag) for the bodies, and appropriate protective gear for such an unpleasant enterprise.

For now, we were exploring the hidden corners to see what type of roofing labour we might need to prepare. A brick edifice protruded into the loft that we assumed was the chimney and made our way carefully around it.

"I wish we'd brought two torches," I groaned.

"Shut up! Come and look here."

Using the brickwork to steady myself, I moved along the side wall.

"I thought this was overly large. Look."

85

Let into the bricks was a crossbeam, leaving a space beneath of about three by six metres. The torchlight revealed a small room containing several wooden boxes. But that was not all, for against the wall was a skeleton.

~~

So that was how a twenty-first century SOCO team came to be scrabbling around in the loft of a cottage, circa 1630s.

Who was it?

I don't know but the bones belonged to a man whose head had been bashed in with an adze similar to the one that had cut the beams.

What was in the boxes?

Ah, that's another one, but those contents had been the death of him.

~~

Later, during the refurbishing, my husband warned me to take care not to fall through the ceiling, to make sure and walk carefully on the crossbeams. However, *he* was the one to put his foot through…Frank Spencer fashion.

That's one of the funnier memories of Old Inn Cottage, but what a mess. Have you ever tried to paint over a lime-washed ceiling? It flakes…and flakes. Then you decide to try and stick paper between the great beams. You start one end, and the paper follows you, falling on your head. Why? Because the flaming ceiling flakes!

~~

Part III

"Watch it!"

Isaac Falcon shouted as Jim Warren stumbled, almost dropping the two brandy bottles as he received them. His hands were sweaty. His whole being was sweaty in the cramped space hidden within the chimney breast that sprouted through the loft of the Inn.

The pair had lugged two casks each, up the steep track leading from Blacksand Creek to the inn on the cliff top. It was a trip they made four times a year. In the cellar, the contents were poured carefully into bottles, corked and taken to the hidden room in the loft. Each bottle was filled exactly to the base of its neck, but the majority already held a couple of inches of water, drawn from the well by Marigold.

A good lass, Marigold, thought Isaac. He had done well for himself when he married her. Her father had controlled smuggling in the area and Isaac now carried out what his father-in-law had previously managed. The old man was a bit shaky these days, legs splayed as though he was permanently astride a horse, his bulbous red-veined nose sprouting hair that helped form a straggling moustache across his top lip. *More there than on his head,* Isaac grinned, a grin that stretched as he visualised the lipless mouth constantly chewing on toothless gums. It wasn't funny though, it was damned annoying. Notwithstanding, the old man could still move like greased lightning when the mood took him. *Old Will 'ud have a fit if he knew I watered the brandy. Straight as a die is Will, but like or lump it, he benefits from the extra cash same as me and there have been no complaints from the Parson and his Lordship.*

"Well, well, what do we 'ave 'ere?"

The booming voice behind him made Isaac jump. It belonged to the revenue man, a large vindictive character who thought highly of himself. *How the hell did he get up here without being noticed? No one knows about the trapdoor in the ceiling, apart from those who should, and the old man should have warned him.*

"Good morning, Mr Lightfoot. I'm just havin' a bit of a clear up, make extra room for when the littl'uns comes along."

Lightfoot drew nearer. Isaac stood before the hidden entrance, hoping that it was indeed well out of sight. "I know what you're up to, Isaac Falcon, and I'm a-gonna put you away for many a year and yer wife and 'er ole man, too."

"No, you're bloody well not," were the last words Lightfoot heard as the adze sliced through his skull. Will was still fast and sure…

A Poetic Break

Now, as they say, for something completely different.

A Donut with Attitude

The catalyst for this poem came from an engineering design my husband was working on. Part of it necessitated a torus and I thought of it as the donut with attitude…I frequently gave his inventions obscure names.

Anyway, this particular phrase caused me to work through the alphabet in my mind to discover rhyming words. I think I have covered most of them, but of course, I'm not infallible.

As a poem, it scans and rhymes to the best of my ability but I would describe it as a prose poem. In fact, it is really just a rather silly bit of fun with words. I must confess, I did enjoy writing it and hope you will enjoy reading it.

Joe Bloggs Last Birthday

I guess I must have heard or read something to do with euthanizing the older generation, which caused me to write this one.

Life Goes On

Definitely inspired by global warming, climate change, and the general state of affairs this world is experiencing nowadays.

A Donut with Attitude

Once upon a time
A Donut of great *Amplitude*
And with an undoubted *Attitude*
Was invented with great *Aptitude*
This Donut with *Attitude*
Did at high *Altitude*
Choose a wife, *BeatItude*
Eventually, they begat *CorrectItude*
Then *ExactItude*
Followed within a year by *FortItude*
And just fifteen months later, *GratItude*
She was just a year old
When *IneptItude* entered the world
Then came the twins, *LatItude* and *LongItude*
Who met *MagnItude and Multitude*
And eventually married them
LatItude and *MagnItude*
Begat triplets *PlatItude, PlenItude* and *PulchrItude*
Also *RectItude*
Whilst *LongItude* and *MultItude*
Begat quadruplets
SolicItude, SolItude, VerisimilItude and *VicissItude*
Thus was formed a Donut family.

WITH ATTITUDE

Joe Bloggs Last Birthday

HE RAN IN THE LONDON MARATHON
ON THE OCCASION OF
HIS SEVENTY-NINTH BIRTHDAY.
THIS YEAR HE WILL NOT RUN,
FOR HE WILL BE ELSEWHERE.
FOR EVERYONE IS NOW RULED
BY THE LATEST EUROPEAN DIRECTIVE
WHEREBY, ON THEIR EIGHTIETH BIRTHDAY
THEY *MUST* ATTEND A SPECIAL CELEBRATION
PROVIDED BY THE GOVERNMENT.
THERE IS CHAMPAGNE AND
A CAKE, BEAUTIFULLY ICED
AND BEARING THE NAME OF
WHOMSOEVER'S BIRTHDAY
IS TO BE CELEBRATED.
TOASTS ARE MADE
IN REMEMBRANCE OF A GOOD LIFE.
THEN THE GUESTS DEPART.
LEAVING JOE
AN ENERGETIC, HEALTHY MAN
WHO LIKES TO RUN MARATHONS
TO DOWN HIS FINAL GLASS OF CHAMPAGNE.
HIS LAST DRINK OF ANYTHING.
FOR JOE BLOGGS IS EIGHTY TODAY
JUST ONE OF TOO MANY ELDERLY FOLK
MOST OF THEM CAPABLE OF LIVING HEALTHILY
WELL INTO THEIR NINETIES AND HUNDREDS.
BUT THE GOVERNMENT IS IN DEBT

SO, IN ITS WISDOM HAS CHOSEN TO
COMPLY WITH THE EU DIRECTIVE
AND THE EUTHANASIA SOCIETY RULES.
SO IF YOU WANT TO LIVE YOUR FULL STRETCH
IN A WAY THAT SUITS YOU, NOT THEM,
THEN RUN, RUN AWAY, HIDE
OR THEY'LL GET YOU TOO.

– Mary Clarke, 2006

Life Goes On

The cows are grazing
In the field at the bottom of our garden
And gossiping
Starlings are an attraction
Ducking, diving in synchronicity, a cloud of birds
A murmuration
Visitors are flying their kites
Arriving in cars with caravans, anticipating happy days
And nights
Distant hills are eclipsed in a sea mist haze
Hopefully bright sunshine, sea and sand will appear
For holidays
On this beautiful blue/green planet
Humanity is threatened by an invisible enemy
A pandemic
This virus can and will mutate
Life will be forever changed so consider carefully
And evaluate

Mary Clarke 2020.